WALKING by FAITH

Five / The Sacraments

Principal Program Consultants

Rev. Terry M. Odien, MA

Rev. Michael D. Place, STD

Dr. Addie Lorraine Walker, SSND

BROWN-ROA

A Division of Harcourt Brace & Company

Nihil Obstat

Rev. Richard L. Schaefer

Censor Librorum

Imprimatur

✠ Most Rev. Jerome Hanus, OSB

Archbishop of Dubuque

September 17, 1997

Feast of Saint Robert Bellarmine, Patron of Catechists

The Ad Hoc Committee to Oversee the Use of the Catechism, National Conference of Catholic Bishops, has found this catechetical series to be in conformity with the *Catechism of the Catholic Church.*

The nihil obstat and imprimatur are official declarations that a book or pamphlet is free of doctrinal or moral error. No implication is contained herein that those who granted the nihil obstat and imprimatur agree with the contents, opinions, or statements expressed.

A Blessing for Beginnings

"So we are always courageous . . .
for we walk by faith. . . ."

—*2 Corinthians 5:6–7*

Leader: This year we come together to
continue our journey of faith.
We are ready to learn from
one another and from our
Church community. And so
we pray:
God of signs and wonders,
be with us on our journey.
Show us your love in our world,
in each other, and
in your Son, Jesus Christ.
And help us be living signs of
your love every day.

Reader: Listen to God's message
to us:
(*Read Isaiah 45:2–8.*)
The word of the Lord.

All: Thanks be to God.

Leader: Let us ask God's blessing on our
journey this year.

All: God—Father, Son, and Holy
Spirit—walk with us.
Open our ears to your message
and our hearts to your love.
Help us grow in wisdom and
understanding,
and keep us in the grace of
your friendship.
We ask this in faith, as we pray
in the words Jesus taught us:
(*Pray the Lord's Prayer.*)

Leader: May the Lord be with us, now
and always.

All: Amen!

WALKING by FAITH

Five / The Sacraments

CHAPTER 1

God Our Creator

PRAYER

God, Creator of all things, help us praise you in wonder and give thanks for being part of creation.

Memorandum

Update!

Condition: Human wonder

Status: Highly contagious

Cause: Unknown, but traces of its presence are everywhere

Victims: People of all ages

Symptoms:

- Condition often begins with curiosity and leads to questions, especially who, why, and how.
- Five senses become extremely sensitive to surroundings.
- Speechlessness sometimes occurs.
- Heart rate increases, but other vital signs remain stable.

Side Effects:

- Respect for life in all forms
- Feelings of appreciation and thankfulness
- Belief in a power beyond human limits

Cure: None known

ACTIVITY

Traces of God's presence are all around us. Make a list of the people and things that remind you of God's presence every day.

A Wonderful Presence

Have you ever experienced wonder? What did you see? How did you feel? Where were you? According to the memorandum, the cause of human wonder is unknown, but traces of its presence are everywhere. When we look at the world around us, we can experience that great presence—in a rainbow painted in the sky, in a dolphin's graceful somersaults above the ocean's surface, in the faces of friends and family. All these things and more lead us to ask who created such beauty.

Catholics believe that **creation**, all things seen and unseen, came to be through God. All creatures are traces or reminders of God's presence and God's gift of life. God alone created the great wonders that are part of our world.

One Creator of All

God did not need help of any kind to create the world and everything in it. All God had to do was command, "Let there be some thing," and it happened. God's word by itself is creative. It is filled with power.

Genesis, the first book of the Bible, answers the question, "Who created all things?" The authors of Genesis answered, "God alone." God alone deserves thanks and praise for everything in the heavens and on the earth.

This answer was **inspired**, or prompted by the Holy Spirit. The inspired writers were so amazed by what God had made, they wrote two stories about the gifts of creation.

The first story of creation explains that in the beginning God created the heavens and the earth. God formed and organized everything. Where there was nothing, God put something. Where there was confusion, God put order (*Genesis 1:1–2*). As God made each thing in creation, he saw how good it was. Each thing, each creature, was good in its own way, but not perfect. Only God was and always is perfect.

After God had created light, day and night, the sky, water, land, vegetables and fruit, the sun, moon, and stars, and all kinds of living creatures, God chose the perfect moment to make a special creature (*Genesis 1:3–26*). God created humans, both men and women, in his own image and likeness (*Genesis 1:27*).

ACTIVITY

God's creation inspires many people to create artwork, such as this painting by Frederic Edwin Church called "Twilight in the Wilderness." Draw a picture of something in creation that inspires you.

Then God did something wonderful. God blessed humans and gave everything to them. This time, when God looked at everything in creation, he found it not just good, but *very* good (*Genesis 1:28–31*).

The second story of creation in Genesis is different from the first. You might say that it is more down-to-earth. In the second story God's work of creation has a personal touch. God is imagined as acting in human ways, like a potter, a gardener, and a matchmaker.

SCRIPTURE STORY
A Special Partner

God formed a man out of clay and blew the breath of life into his nostrils, making him a living being. Then God planted a garden and placed the man there. To keep the man company, God made all kinds of living creatures. But when God saw that none of these creatures was just right for the man, God made him a special partner. God created a woman from one of the man's ribs. God brought the first man and the first woman together in a beautiful union of love. In God's eyes they were made for each other.

—*based on Genesis 2:7–24*

We are all God's children. God created us out of love. How can we share in the love God has for us?

Stories of Faith and Wonder

The stories of creation in the Bible are not scientific explanations of how the world came to be. People living at the time the Book of Genesis was written did not have textbooks or tools such as microscopes and telescopes to study the world around them. They trusted their five senses and their own observations and imagination. These were their ways of knowing and describing the world.

The authors of Genesis were moved by God to write what they did about creation. The creation stories are filled with faith and wonder. Their main purpose is to show God's power and glory as Creator of all things.

- **Why do you think God chose human authors to tell about creation?**

Landmark Scribes and artists *illuminated*, or illustrated, the Bible to celebrate God's power and glory and to express their faith and awe. This illuminated page from the Book of Genesis tells the first story of creation.

Understanding Scripture

In Scripture God speaks to us through human authors. When we read the Bible, we need to pay attention to what God is telling us through the words of humans.

Here are steps to follow:

- Read the passage slowly and prayerfully with an open heart and mind.

- Remember that the Bible is God's word written in human words.

- Keep in mind that although the authors of the Bible wrote at a particular time and place, their inspired message has meaning for all time.

- Recall that every passage in the Bible reveals God's plan for us: to come to know, love, and serve God in this life and be happy with him in heaven.

- Always pause and reflect on what the passage means to you at the moment.

- Remind yourself that your personal understanding of a passage in the Bible is not the final understanding.

- Bear in mind that the Bible is the Church's book and that the Church interprets and teaches how we can faithfully follow God's word.

Where Will This Lead Me?

Practicing these steps will help you feel comfortable reading Scripture and thinking about its meaning.

RECALL

Who created all things, seen and unseen? What book in the Bible tells about creation?

THINK AND SHARE

Which of the two stories of creation in the Bible appeals to you more? Why?

CONTINUE THE JOURNEY

Imagine that you are a scientist. You have been invited to give a talk about how faith and science can work together to take care of creation. Make some notes for your talk.

WE LIVE OUR FAITH

At Home   Volunteer to pray a prayer before a family meal. Thank God for the gifts of creation, including the food you are about to eat.

In the Parish   At Mass, pay special attention to the prayers, readings, and songs that praise God the Creator. Find out how members of your faith community show reverence for creation, and join in if you can.

Bless the Lord

The Book of Daniel in the Bible tells the story of three faithful Israelites. They were thrown into a white-hot furnace for refusing to worship a golden statue set up by the Babylonian king Nebuchadnezzar. Instead of dying in the flames, the three men were heard singing the praises of God, the Creator of heaven and earth. Stunned that they were still alive, the king ordered everyone to worship the true God who delivered the men from certain death (*Daniel 3:1–97*).

The beautiful hymn the three men sang is called the **Benedicite**, which means "bless" in Latin. The Benedicite is a song of faith in God as Creator. The phrase "bless the Lord" is repeated many times in the hymn as the singers invite different parts of creation to join them in praising God.

PRAYER

As a class, praise God the Creator of heaven and earth by praying all or part of the Benedicite (*Daniel 3:52–90*).

CHAPTER 2

Signs of God's Love

PRAYER

God, signs of your love are everywhere in creation. We turn to you for help. Let us be living signs of your loving care in the world.

"We missed the sign." We groan when we hear those words. When we double back, we spot the sign immediately and wonder how we could have missed it in the first place. Weren't we paying attention?

Throughout our faith journey there are signs that point to God's presence in our lives. These signs are everywhere so that we do not miss coming to know, love, and serve God. Each sign is a **revelation**—that is, each is a part of the gradual process through which we come to know God. God shows us the way because he loves us. Even so, we sometimes do not see the signs. We become so busy that we do not look around or beyond ourselves. When this happens, we may lose sight of God's love. We may lose our way.

ACTIVITY

Make a reminder to pay attention to signs of God's love around you.

SCRIPTURE STORY
Turn to God

One day Jesus was enjoying a few moments to himself on a beautiful hillside. Before he knew it, a crowd of people had gathered around him and started to pour their hearts out to him about their cares and worries.

"What are we going to eat?" "What are we going to drink?" "What are we going to wear?" they asked.

Jesus listened. Then he said, "Look at the birds in the air, the flowers waving in the fields! They are dressed in beauty and color that no one can match. They do not work or worry, but God takes care of them. Are you not more important than they are? How much more will God provide for you if you have faith and trust! Do not be bothered with useless worries about what you are going to eat, drink, or wear. Your heavenly Father knows exactly what you need. Look for God's love and goodness at work in your life, and all the rest will be given to you."

—based on Matthew 6:25–33

Jesus was telling the people to stop and look around them. Stop being blind to the signs of God's love. Look at nature and how God takes care of it. Open yourself to God's love. Trust in God. If you depend on God instead of trying to do everything by yourself, you will have what you really need.

Saints Walk with Us

Saint Patrick
Feast Day: March 17

Saint Patrick saw God's love in the wonders of creation.

Legend says that Saint Patrick used the shamrock to teach about the Holy Trinity.

Signs Along Our Way

It happens almost every day. A desperate family makes an urgent plea for blood or bone marrow that will save a dying child's life. Often, as time is running out, a donor walks into a blood bank or hospital. This kind of human gesture is a sign of God's love and goodness in the world. It is a life-giving action that reflects the love and goodness of the Creator of all life. Through such acts we show that life is a precious gift from God that we can share with one another.

God has given us many other gifts. God's love and goodness also shine through in nature, for instance. We can experience the wonders of nature when we go hiking or camping or when we take a walk down the street or sit in a park. Away from the comforts of home or just out from the indoors, the rough edges of less familiar surroundings brush up against our senses, especially our eyes, ears, and noses.

ACTIVITY

There are many ways that we can show each other that life is a gift from God. Draw a picture of someone sharing the gift of life.

Why do you think many people feel especially close to God when they are in nature?

Perhaps for the first time, we see how important the sun is as a source of light and nourishment. As we listen to the sounds that birds and other animals make, we start to see these creatures, too, as signs of God's love and goodness. As we breathe in the air, we meet all kinds of smells—fresh, musty, sweet, sharp. All these are signs of life and of God's love.

Yet we do not have to travel far to discover signs of God's love for us. Our family and friends are the closest living signs pointing to God. They are clear signs of love that we cannot miss. They show us every day that God is the source of everything that is good in life.

Scripture Signpost

"The heavens declare the glory of God;
the sky proclaims its builder's craft."

Psalm 19:2

Where else besides the heavens or sky can we look to see God's glory and creativity?

Our Moral Guide

Freedom is the power to choose. We are responsible for our actions. We are free to choose to act responsibly toward God and other people.

Catechism, #1731

What might keep people from freely choosing to do good?

These children lost their home in a hurricane. Where can we turn when bad things happen?

Losing Our Way

We do not question that God's goodness and beauty shine through all of what is good and beautiful in the world. But when we see pain and suffering in people's lives, we wonder where they come from. Catholics firmly believe that God, who is the source of all that is good in the world, does not cause evil. **Evil**, the opposite of God's good plan for creation, comes about as a result of sin.

Sometimes on our faith journey, we miss the signs and get lost. We were created to share in God's goodness and love. Our choice to turn away from God's invitation is called **sin**. Sin does not come from God. It comes from the human heart and mind *(Psalm 64:6; Matthew 15:19)*. Sin is original with us. In other words, the origins or roots of sin lie within our nature as humans. The first humans chose to disobey, to turn away from God. That is why we speak of **original sin**.

Because of sin, our relationships with God, with ourselves, and with others suffer. Sin and the suffering that goes with it can blind our hearts, minds, and senses, so that we cannot see the signs of God's goodness and beauty. Instead we experience a gigantic ache for what is missing—our friendship with creation and, through it, with God, who is all good.

Even though sin and evil exist, there are many signs of God's love in creation. All encourage us to reflect on what is good and beautiful in the world and to seek happiness in God, the giver of all good gifts. Six signs, or symbols, in particular have special meaning.

Rainbow God set a rainbow in the clouds after the Great Flood and promised never again to destroy the earth and all living creatures by water. Every rainbow recalls that promise.

Light With light God shattered the darkness. Christ, the Light of the World, brings us out of the darkness of sin and overcomes evil and suffering in his dying and rising.

Water God made water life-giving. In the water of Baptism, we are reborn, and sin is washed away.

Symbols of God's Love

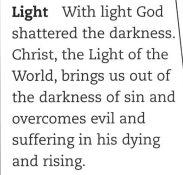

Mountains Created to tower over us, mountains are a symbol of God's greatness. God gave us the Commandments and Jesus gave us the Beatitudes on mountains.

Desert God led people into the desert to speak to them. The desert is a symbol of stillness and silence, where we learn to depend on God's word, not human words.

Fields From the grains gathered in the fields, God gives us food. Fields are a symbol of the Bread of Life that we receive in the Eucharist.

RECALL

Who is the source of all that is good in the world? Where does evil come from?

THINK AND SHARE

What person, event, or thing would you name as a sign of God's love and goodness in the world? Explain your choice.

CONTINUE THE JOURNEY

Look inside yourself and draw two contrasting pictures. First, draw a time when you chose to turn away from the invitation to share God's goodness and love. Then, next to it, draw what you might have done instead if you had not turned away.

WE LIVE OUR FAITH

At Home Think of a way you can be a sign of God's love to each member of your family. Try out your ideas this week.

In the Parish Share God's loving care with another student in your parish. Ask your teacher or the head of your school if volunteer tutors are needed. Tutor a younger student who needs help with schoolwork.

Let Us Become Signs

Whenever we gather together to pray and to work, we believe that God is with us. We show our trust in God by building new parishes, founding schools and hospitals, and running soup kitchens and youth centers. We donate food, clothing, and money when natural disasters strike or there is some other need. These activities are signs of faith and spring from our belief that God will provide for all of creation.

Pray that we may show our concern for others and become signs that God continues to watch over all people.

PRAYER

**God our Creator,
we are the work of your hands.
Guide us in our work,
that we may do it, not for self alone,
but for the common good.
Make us alert to injustice,
ready to stand in solidarity,
that there may be dignity for all
in labor and in labor's reward.**

CHAPTER 3

Caring for God's Creation

PRAYER

God, you invite us to share in your plan for creation. Help us be responsible caretakers of the blessings of your creation.

A lonely scientist walked along a crowded beach. Her head was spinning with questions and doubts. How long would this planet survive?

As she walked, she noticed beachcombers scavenging for conchs, coral, and starfish. Later they would sell what they had found. Then she spied the "star thrower." Instead of collecting the dying starfish, the stranger was throwing them back into the sea. The scientist and the stranger did not have to speak. Both knew what had to be done.

The scientist joined the "star thrower," flinging the starfish back into the sea. Her worries seemed to drift away with the tide. In their place hope began to well up. The scientist knew that starfish tossed back into the ocean had a chance to survive. If more people like the "star thrower" would step forward, maybe all creation would have that same chance.

- **Why will there always be a need for new "star throwers"?**

God Calls Us to Care

From the first moment of creation, God has been calling us to care for the gifts of creation. Like the star thrower and the scientist, we can say yes to God's invitation to care. Our simple actions can renew the earth. When we use water wisely, recycle paper, or throw trash in a bin instead of on the ground, we are answering God's call to honor the earth.

The first people to live in the land that is our home today knew how to honor creation. Some Native Americans believed that the land and what they harvested from it came from the sun god they called the Great Spirit. Because they believed this, these Native Americans treated the earth with respect and tried to use it wisely. We are coming to learn the same simple truth. The water and the land belong not to us, who use them, but to God, who made them (*Psalm 95:5*). It is up to us to care for what God has entrusted to us.

Scripture Signpost

"For creation awaits with eager expectation the revelation of the children of God."
Romans 8:19

Who are the children of God? Why is creation eager for the revelation of the children of God?

ACTIVITY

God has given creation into our care. With a partner, make a checklist of ways we can protect the gifts of creation.

A Plan for Creation

There is no magic in our doing and caring on this earth. We are part of a plan that God has for all creation. God's plan, called **providence**, is gradually unfolding. God makes this plan known through the loving care and guidance he offers to all creatures. We can see signs of God's providence in our own lives when we look through the eyes of faith at things that have happened to us. When we do this, we begin to understand why certain things occurred. We begin to see how things may have actually worked out for our own good.

Although God is in charge of the plan for creation, we are meant to help carry out the plan through our actions. When God created us, he gave us responsibility for the rest of creation (*Genesis 1:26–28*). When we act for the good of creation, God's invisible power is working through us, and we are helping fulfill God's plan.

ACTIVITY

This boy is working in a community garden. From the checklist you made with your partner, choose one way you can protect creation. Draw a picture of yourself taking on this responsibility.

Jesus Carried Out God's Plan

God's Son became human in Jesus. Jesus came into the world in order to carry out God's plan for creation. In becoming truly one of us, Jesus turned the world upside down. Where people believed in magic and false gods, Jesus offered faith and signs of a living and caring God. Above all, Jesus asked for a change of heart among people. Instead of getting and holding onto things, Jesus said, people should let go and not cling. He tried to make them see that life is not made up of possessions (*Luke 12:15*).

Those who listened to Jesus saw that he practiced what he preached. To carry out God's will, Jesus left a safe, comfortable life in a village. He chose a life of teaching and good acts, traveling about with no place to rest his head. Jesus cured and healed people. When he saw hungry people, he fed them. He never asked for anything in return, only for faith in God.

Jesus trusted in God's providence, God's loving and caring plan for all creatures. Jesus saw that people continued to worry about many things. He understood that their cares were real to them, but he knew that they did not have to worry (*Matthew 6:31–33*). Jesus helped carry out God's plan by trying to convince people to depend on God, who would care for all their needs.

In what he said and did, Jesus showed how to care for God's creation. Why do you think Jesus told people not to worry?

We Do Our Part

We are reminded that we can depend on God by a simple phrase in the Lord's Prayer. In the words "Give us this day our daily bread," we understand that God will give us what we need. But once we receive what we need, it is time for us to do our part. It is time for us to share and give with an open hand and heart. In doing so, we show **stewardship**, or responsible care, for God's creation.

As good stewards, or caretakers, of God's creation, we have the opportunity to be creative. To be creative means to do ordinary things with extraordinary care. We can show our stewardship at home by loving and helping our families. We can show responsibility outside our homes for people who are homeless and hungry. Every day we can take care of the earth by using resources wisely and respecting other living creatures. There are many ways we can share in God's creating.

How is this child caring for creation?

Caring for Creation

When we care for any part of God's creation, we understand that we are sharing in God's love and care for all creation.

Here are steps to follow:

- Remember that your caring action is a sign of God's providence at work here and now.
- Start small and close to home to do some good.
- Choose an action whose effects will be felt for a long time, not an action that provides a quick fix and may be undone just as quickly.
- Work with others who have experience doing worthwhile projects.
- Respect the feelings, rights, and property of other people.
- Expect people to ask how your actions will affect their lives directly or indirectly.

- Be sure that what you do creates feelings of cooperation and goodwill rather than tension and conflict.
- Keep asking yourself questions as you go along.
- Finish what you start to do.
- Follow up and evaluate what has been done.
- Honor your work by asking God to bless what you have been enabled to do in his name.

Where Will This Lead Me?

Following these steps will help you make a positive contribution and encourage you to continue to care for God's creation.

RECALL

What is God's providence? What is our part in God's plan for creation?

THINK AND SHARE

How did Jesus' care for creation reflect God's care for creation?

CONTINUE THE JOURNEY

Using each letter in the word STEWARDSHIP as a first letter, write ten other words that tell what stewardship means to you. (The word *HELP* is shown as a guide.) When you are finished, explain to a partner how each word is connected to the idea of stewardship.

STEWARDSHIP

S — share
T — trust
E — earth
W — acting to help
A — action
R — responsibility
D — over
S — stewardship
H — HELP
E — E
L — L
P — P
I — se
P — provedence

WE LIVE OUR FAITH

At Home Think of ways you can use water more wisely. Practice your ideas at home this week.

In the Parish Another meaning of *stewardship* is sharing material things as a faith community. During the week, save what money you can to donate to the collection at Mass.

Caring Gifts

At every Eucharist we show our care for God's creation in an important action called the **Presentation of the Gifts.** Among the gifts brought to the altar by representatives from the assembly are the bread and wine to be consecrated.

Along with these offerings are gifts of money from people gathered at Mass. In making these donations, Catholics share what they have earned from their work in offices, factories, and other businesses. With their offerings they make a cheerful and willing sacrifice in thanksgiving for God's blessing. Their caring gifts are important to the parish and diocese because money helps the Church continue to reach out and serve people, especially those in need.

PRAYER

As a group, recite the Beatitudes given in Matthew 5:3–12. After each Beatitude, respond "God loves a cheerful giver."

Parish Car Wash

FEED THE HUNGRY

Review

Multiple Choice Write the letter of the choice that best completes the sentence.

_b_ 1. God created all things **(a)** to be perfect **(b)** without any help **(c)** including evil **(d)** in God's image and likeness.

_c_ 2. Sin comes from **(a)** creation **(b)** God **(c)** the human heart and mind **(d)** evil.

_d_ 3. Jesus helped carry on God's plan by **(a)** worrying about others **(b)** living a comfortable life **(c)** letting go of possessions **(d)** trying to convince people to trust God.

_b_ 4. The main purpose of the creation stories in the Bible is to **(a)** offer a scientific explanation of the world **(b)** show God's power and glory as the Creator of all things **(c)** describe the world **(d)** inspire the authors of Genesis.

_c_ 5. Mountains are symbols of **(a)** Baptism **(b)** the Mass **(c)** God's greatness **(d)** stewardship.

Fill in the Blanks Complete each sentence with the correct term.

1. Our name for all things seen and unseen is _creation_ .

2. We can see signs of God's _presence_ in the loving care and guidance God offers us and in the events of our lives.

3. Our responsibility to take care of God's gift of creation is called _stewardship_

4. God's plan is called _providence_.

5. _sin_ is the choice we make to turn away from God's love.

Share Your Faith Imagine that you are the youngest member of a space mission. You have been asked to broadcast a message to young people on earth about the beauty of creation and our responsibility for it. What will you say?

Show How Far You've Come

Use this chart to show what you have learned. For each chapter, write the three most important things you remember.

Creation Celebrates God's Love

Chapter 1 God Our Creator	Chapter 2 Signs of God's Love	Chapter 3 Caring for God's Creation

What Else Would You Like to Know?

List any questions you still have about God's creation and how we share in it.

_____

_____

_____

Continue the Journey

Choose one or more of the following activities to do on your own, with your class, or with your family.

- Look through your Faith Journal pages for Unit One. Choose your favorite activity and share it with a friend or family member.

- Make a collage of signs of God's love in creation. Use pictures clipped from old magazines or your own drawings in your collage. Ask your teacher if you can post your collage in the classroom or share it with the rest of the class.

- Plan a project that will show love and care for creation. Ask an adult for help in planning or carrying out the project you have in mind. After completing your project, evaluate what you did, and write a short report that summarizes both your goals and the results of your work.

Sign of the New Creation

PRAYER

Mary, your whole being praises God in heaven. Lead us home to share eternal life with God as you do through your glorious assumption.

Have you noticed? Advertisers are everywhere, and they want you. They want you to believe that they can create a "new" you. They tell you that if you wear their jeans, you will have a certain image. If you wear their sneakers, you'll become a sports star. If you use their beauty product, overnight you'll become someone different. And if you choose a certain school or career, you can become an even better and richer person than you are.

What do you think? Is there really something wrong with the "image" you already have? Look in the mirror. What do you see?

We need to remind ourselves that God, and only God, is our Creator. We do not create our image, nor does anyone or anything else. We were created in God's image and likeness. We exist through the loving power of God.

There will be many people—parents, teachers, coaches—who will give some shape and direction to your life. Ultimately, however, it will be up to you to decide who you are and who you want to be. Trusting yourself as a person made in the image and likeness of God is part of that process.

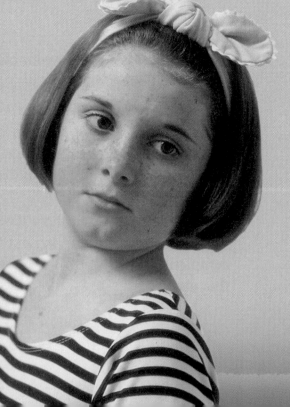

Catholics Believe . . .
that Mary was taken into heaven body and soul.

Catechism, #966

This painting shows one artist's view of Mary being welcomed into heaven by her son. How does Mary give us hope?

We Look to Mary in Hope

Mary, the mother of Jesus Christ, is an example to us of the loving power of God. God favored Mary with special gifts. Through God's power Mary was full of grace. From the very beginning of Mary's existence, her **soul**, the immortal part of her being, was free of sin. Mary's whole life was centered on her son, the Son of God, Jesus Christ. At the end of her life on earth, Mary was taken into heaven body and soul. We celebrate this great event as Mary's **assumption**, or "being taken up."

Special love and devotion to Mary are an important part of who we are as Catholics. Even though the Bible does not describe what happened to Mary at the end of her life, Catholics have always trusted that she was reunited with her son. The **doctrine**, or formal teaching, of the assumption was proclaimed within the last century, in 1950. But people around the world have been celebrating a feast day in honor of the assumption from the earliest years of the Church.

Mary is the first person to share in Christ's resurrection. Through her assumption Mary is fully and completely with the risen Christ. By celebrating and honoring Mary, we show our belief that we, too, will share, body and soul, in the glory of Christ's resurrection.

RECALL

What is the assumption? Why is Mary's assumption important to us?

THINK AND SHARE

Why do you think people are interested in the details of Mary's life that aren't in the Bible?

CONTINUE THE JOURNEY

In the mirror, draw your very best self—the person, body and soul, that you are called to be.

WE LIVE OUR FAITH

At Home Show respect for your whole being—body and soul—and that of family members by doing one thing to improve your family's physical and spiritual health.

In the Parish Find out how your parish honors Mary. Participate in prayers or celebrations in Mary's honor.

Lead Us Home

In the prayer called the *Salve, Regina*—Latin for "Hail, Holy Queen"—we make a special appeal to Mary. We salute her as Queen of heaven and earth, but we also call to her as one of us. Like us, Mary is a child of Eve. Through her assumption Mary has gone before us to heaven, our true home. With the words of the *Salve, Regina*, we ask Mary to lead us home to heaven and eternal life with Jesus Christ.

Pray the *Salve, Regina* together.

Prayer

Hail, holy Queen, Mother of mercy,
hail, our life, our sweetness, and our hope.
To you we cry, the children of Eve,
to you we send up our sighs,
mourning and weeping in this land of exile.
Turn, then, most gracious advocate,
your eyes of mercy toward us;
lead us home at last
and show us the blessed fruit of your
    womb, Jesus.
O clement, O loving, O sweet Virgin Mary.

CHAPTER 5

We All Seek God

PRAYER

**God, fill our restless hearts with your loving kindness.
Teach us to find our happiness in you.**

The newborn cupped and cradled in a palm feels that
touch, the human touch.
The infant held and nursed at the breast senses that
touch, the human touch.
The child hugged and kissed in an embrace enjoys that
touch, the human touch.
The teen loved and loving in new ways seeks that touch,
the human touch.
The adult giving and receiving that touch knows by heart
and mind somehow that
touch is divine.

ACTIVITY

**Imagine what each
of the people shown
is communicating
through touch. Then
write a caption for
each picture.**

The Human Touch

If there is one thing that we all crave as humans, it is to be touched by people who love us. Touch helps us connect with each other and makes us feel alive. Without it we fade and droop. Abandoned infants have been observed to lie motionless in their hospital cribs because no one touched them, held them, or talked to them. But when nurses began to pick them up on a regular basis and hold and touch them, the infants responded with smiles, had heartier appetites, and became more active.

In a very real way, the human touch is a revelation. It is part of the process through which we come to know God. But the power of the human touch to heal and satisfy is limited. It points to something more, something beyond our senses. Somewhere the true source of all human happiness waits for us. To find it, we reach out with our bodies, our minds, and our spirits. We discover that the something more beyond our senses is God. As believers, we want to be in touch with God and to be touched by God.

Scripture Signpost

"O God, you are my God—for you I long! For you my body yearns; for you my soul thirsts."

Psalm 63:2

Why do you think we seek God?

20th century, French

10th century, Greek

People continue to see the human face of God in Jesus. Artists show Jesus as a person of their own time and culture.

Catholics Believe . . .

that we find true happiness only in God.

Catechism, #27

Where Is God?

When Jesus began his life of ministry, his homeland of Judea was part of the powerful Roman Empire. Ordinary people—farmers and laborers—suffered a great deal. They had to pay high taxes to the Romans and obey their orders. People had no hope because they could see no relief from their troubles in the future. They looked everywhere for signs of God's care in their lives. The poor and the suffering came to such a point of despair that they asked, "Where is our God?"

With Us in Jesus

The Gospels tell us that Jesus' preaching and the many wonderful things he did gave people hope. Jesus touched the hearts of many. People were amazed at what Jesus said and did. They believed that he had been sent by God to save them. Not everyone in the crowd was sure of this, however. Some people did not see God in Jesus. They doubted that Jesus came from God.

Show Us the Father

Even Jesus' most trusted friends, his apostles, sometimes did not understand him. On the night that Jesus was betrayed by his friend Judas, the apostles still did not completely grasp who Jesus really was.

That night Jesus told his friends that he was going away, but he promised to return. The apostles were frightened and begged to know where he was going. Desperate for a clear sign, the apostle Philip said to Jesus, "Master, show us the Father, and that will be enough for us."

Jesus saw right away that the apostles still did not know who he was. To calm their troubled hearts, he explained, "Whoever has seen me has seen the Father."

—*based on John 14:8–9*

ACTIVITY

The apostles were afraid and asked Jesus for reassurance. Tell a story or draw a picture of a time when you were afraid and needed reassurance or comfort.

● **What do you think Jesus meant when he told the apostles, "Whoever has seen me has seen the Father"?**

Growing Closer to God

By sending Jesus to heal and save us, God answered the question "Where are you, God?" Jesus is the perfect **image of God**. He shows God's love for us fully and completely. In fact, the name *Emmanuel,* which is used to describe Jesus, means "God is with us" (*Matthew 1:23*). Jesus made God present and alive among the people of our world. In his life of ministry, Jesus set out to love, create, and forgive—to show that God is with us.

Faith is the power that enables us to believe that God is with us. Faith also helps us respond to God's presence in our lives. We receive the gift of faith in the Sacrament of Baptism. Washed and reborn in the waters of Baptism, we become children of God and members of the Body of Christ.

Baptism is just the beginning of our faith journey. Our faith grows and develops as we do. We come to know God through creation and through the Bible. We see God in Jesus. Along the way we also find help from parents and others who believe. The faith of the Church community helps us on our journey of faith.

ACTIVITY

When did you receive the gift of faith? Write a short description of your own Baptism.

Listening to God

When we **meditate**, or pray and reflect, we seek God within ourselves through the gateways of our senses.

Here are some steps to follow:

- Sit quietly. Put yourself in God's hands. Remember that God is the one trying to reach you and touch your heart. Let go of noise, questions, and answers in your thoughts. Open all of your senses to God's presence.

- Imagine yourself as a half-finished drawing or piece of sculpture that God is going to finish. Let God begin to work on you.

- Think of your desire to be with God. Repeat God's name in your mind as you call to God.

- Let God speak to you. Listen with your heart and mind. Open your hand as a sign that your heart and mind are open to God's influence.

- End your time of meditation by thanking God for always being with you. Say "Amen."

Where Will This Lead Me?

Practicing these steps will help you develop a way of meditating that works for you and will encourage you to seek God on a daily basis.

RECALL

In what sacrament do we receive the gift of faith? What happens in that sacrament?

THINK AND SHARE

What kinds of events teach us that God is the source of true happiness?

CONTINUE THE JOURNEY

We can think of our community of faith as a chain. Each person in the chain helps others believe. In each link of the chain, write the name of someone who has helped you on your journey of faith.

Mom   dad   brother   priest   C.C.D. teacher

WE LIVE OUR FAITH

At Home   Create an image of faith that would be instantly recognized by other people in your family. The image might be as simple as a cross drawn on a sheet of paper and displayed on the refrigerator door.

In the Parish   During the Communion Rite at Mass, extend the sign of peace to all those around you. Think of your human touch as a sign of God's presence.

We Gather to Praise God

The faithful come together at the **Mass**, a sacred meal of sacrifice and praise to God. In the Mass God welcomes us with the words of the Scriptures and is with us in the Eucharist. Through the different parts of the Mass, the Holy Spirit shapes a parish community in the image of Christ's Body, the Church. No matter who we are, poor or rich, young or old, our presence is important in that gathering.

Praise the greatness and goodness of God by praying these words from Psalm 145.

PRAYER

You, LORD, are near to all who call upon you,
   to all who call upon you in truth.
You satisfy the desire of those who fear you;
   you hear their cry and save them.
You, LORD, watch over all who love you.
My mouth will speak your praises, LORD;
   all flesh will bless your holy name forever.

—Psalm 145:18–21

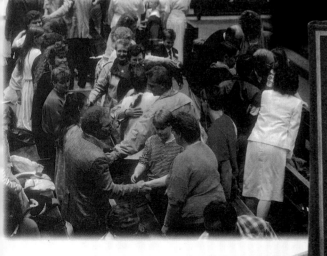

CHAPTER 6
In Prayer and Worship

PRAYER

**God our Father, move our hearts to worship you.
Send your Holy Spirit to lead us in our song of praise.**

Whether called *Oma*, *Abuelita*, or Grandma, a grandmother is often the loving center of a family. Grandmothers can pull the family together and include everyone. They can also make us feel that we stand out as individuals, that we are special by ourselves and for ourselves.

Grandmothers make sure that none of us gets lost in the bustle of family gatherings. At Grandma's the place of honor is not at the head of the table. It is in Grandma's lap. No matter how many children climb into Grandma's lap, there is always room for one more. There Grandma shows us love, makes us laugh, and teaches us.

The "Grandma" in your life may be a parent or godparent, an uncle or a sister, a neighbor, or a friend. Whatever name you know her or him by, this person teaches you what it means to receive love and return it. This person becomes for you a powerful sign of God, who is love.

ACTIVITY

Make a list of ways your grandmother or some other family member has taught you how to show love.

To Honor God

We do *learn* to love because we are loved first. We learn to believe because someone has faith in us. Loving and believing are ways of responding. Members of our own families and of our family of faith—the Church—teach us. Through them we come to know that God loves us and believes in us.

Scripture Signpost

"Take care to keep my sabbaths, for that is to be the token between you and me."

Exodus 31:13

Sabbath is the Hebrew word for "the Lord's day," the weekly time of worship and rest. Why do you think people need to be reminded of their duty to worship God?

Why do you think it is important for people to worship God as a community?

Prayer and worship are ways that we respond to God's love and God's gift of faith. We honor God through **prayer**, lifting up our hearts and minds in love. We also honor God through **worship**, offering words and actions in public praise and thanks. The Third Commandment reminds us that we have a duty to worship God. But that duty is also a joy and a gift. Spending time with someone who loves us, someone we love very much, is never a chore. So that we have time to worship God, we must avoid unnecessary work on the Lord's day and be rested in mind and body.

There is a time and place for individual acts of worship in the Catholic Church. At the heart of our worship, however, is the community of faith. We pray and worship together. When we pray and worship as a body, or group, we multiply our response. There is more love and more faith to go around.

Our Work Is God's Work

There is a reason we are called to worship God as a community. The God whom we worship is, in a sense, a community: the **Holy Trinity** of Father, Son, and Holy Spirit. Our worship community is a reflection of the Trinity.

The public, official worship of the Church is called **liturgy**, from a Greek word that means "the work of the people." The liturgy is our work, or action, of worshiping God as a community. But liturgy is God's work, too. As we offer our response of love and faith to God, God offers us even more.

In the liturgy God our Father and Creator acts to save us. Jesus, the Son of God, our Redeemer, acts to offer himself to the Father for us and with us. The Holy Spirit, our Sanctifier, acts to bless us and make us holy. So liturgy is not only something we do for God, but something God does with and for us.

Worship Makes a Difference

We most often participate in liturgy through the Mass. The Eucharist is the center and heart of our liturgical life, the very best form of worship. We are also participating in liturgy when we celebrate the other sacraments or join in the Church's public daily prayer.

Landmark Different Catholic communities celebrate the liturgy in different ways. In Eastern Catholic churches an icon screen divides the altar from the rest of the church. The doors in the screen are a sign that the liturgy is a doorway, or meeting place, connecting us with God.

The key word is *participate*. We participate in worship when we are fully present for prayer and liturgy. That means bringing our whole selves to meet with God. If our bodies are at Mass but our hearts and minds are elsewhere, we aren't participating. The worshiping community needs all of us, not just the priest and other liturgical ministers.

Prayer and liturgy are languages for communicating with God. Learning to worship means learning this language. It means learning prayers and responses by heart. It means knowing when to listen in silence and when to sing out joyfully. The language of worship means understanding the symbols we use in celebration. It means being comfortable with postures and gestures for prayer, like kneeling or making the Sign of the Cross.

Learning how to worship God in prayer and liturgy makes a difference in our lives. If we actively participate, the Mass may not seem boring. Worship will not be something we *have* to do, but something we *want* to do, because it brings us closer to God and to one another.

ACTIVITY

List three things about the Mass that you would like to know more about. How could knowing more about these things make you a better participant in worship?

SCRIPTURE STORY
Jesus Shows the Way

Our Moral Guide

The word *Mass* comes from the Latin word for "sending forth." Liturgy sends us out to serve God's people in our everyday lives. That service is another way to worship God.

Catechism, #1332

How is serving people a kind of worship?

What do you think Jesus was teaching his friends by washing their feet?

Jesus' friends loved to eat supper with him. He had a way of praying the traditional blessings of the food with great care. It was as though God were at the table with them. The ancient words and gestures had special meaning.

But one evening Jesus surprised his friends. As they sat together around the table, Jesus stood up and took off his outer robe. He wrapped a towel around his waist, took a pitcher of water and a large bowl, and started to wash his friends' feet. Jesus' friends were shocked. What was he thinking? Foot washing was a sign of hospitality, reserved for rich and powerful guests. Jesus' friends had never been welcomed this way. Even if they had felt worthy, foot washing was something that servants did! Yet here was Jesus, their beloved teacher and friend, honoring them as though they were special.

"You don't understand what I am doing now," Jesus said. There was sadness in his eyes, even as he smiled at his friends with great love. "But you will understand later. I am doing this for you now as a model. As I have done this for you, do it for one another."

—based on John 13:4–15

Planning a Prayer Service

We are encouraged to gather anywhere and at anytime to pray. One good way to learn more about prayer and liturgy is to plan your own prayer service. Participating in worship is especially meaningful when you have contributed to the celebration.

Here are some steps to follow:

- Decide on a specific theme or purpose for the gathering.
- Make sure the place set aside for the prayer service is comfortable. Check to see what activities will be going on nearby and how much privacy your group will have.
- Select a prayer leader and readers. Ask them to prepare their prayers and readings in advance of the gathering.

- If you wish, use appropriate audiovisual aids such as music and videotapes to stimulate and inspire those taking part.
- Reserve a place of honor for the Bible as the word of God in your midst.
- Allow time during the service for quiet meditation on the prayers and readings.
- Try to include a gesture, such as the sign of peace, that will reinforce the theme of the service.

Where Will This Lead Me?

Following these steps will help increase your appreciation of group prayer and will make you more aware of occasions for prayer.

RECALL

What is liturgy? What do we call the one God who is Father, Son, and Holy Spirit?

THINK AND SHARE

What are some things that keep people your age from participating in liturgy? How would you help someone your age participate more fully in liturgy?

CONTINUE THE JOURNEY

Worship is an activity in which all members of the Church take part. Draw a picture that shows how you participate in the liturgy.

WE LIVE OUR FAITH

At Home Compose a prayer, or ask to lead your family in a prayer.

In the Parish Find out from a parish staff member how young people can participate more fully in worship. Young people may be encouraged to become altar servers or choir members or to act as lectors or ushers.

We Sing to Your Glory

We are never alone when we worship God. Our prayer and liturgy join us with one another. And they join us with all people, in all times and places, who have ever worshiped God.

Even the unseen parts of God's creation join in our prayer. The **angels,** beings of pure spirit who serve as God's messengers, praise God continually. Our earthly liturgy echoes the song of angels.

Join with all creation to praise the Holy Trinity in prayer.

PRAYER

You gather us into your Church to be one,
as you, Father, are one with your Son
　　and the Holy Spirit.
You call us to be your people,
to praise your wisdom in all your works.
You make us the Body of Christ
and the dwelling-place of the Holy Spirit.
In our joy we sing to your glory with all the
　　choirs of angels!

—based on Preface VIII for Sundays in Ordinary Time

CHAPTER 7

God in Us

PRAYER

God, your Spirit filled us with new life in the waters of Baptism. Continue that new life in us, your children, and help us become more like you.

While many students in the fifth grade had braces on their teeth, Clare had braces on her legs. Yet what made Clare different was not her braces but her courage. During recess or gym, she never just sat on the sidelines. One moment, she was cheering her classmates on to victory. The next, she was blowing her whistle and calling fouls as a no-nonsense referee. What they did, she did. No questions asked, no excuses given.

Clare's greatest triumph was not in walking again without braces—she never did. No, her triumph was in learning how to dance. For someone who avoided leaning on anyone, being held by someone on a dance floor was very difficult. Yet, after the first few steps, Clare's look of fear disappeared, and a broad smile flashed across her face like a bright neon sign.

Learning to Live and to Lean

Clare was a person of spirit. She taught her classmates that everyone, no matter what challenges he or she faces, wants to live life to the full. She showed those around her that there are many ways to do just that. Through acts of courage Clare and her classmates dared to say no to pity and despair and yes to encouragement and enthusiasm. They treated each day as a gift to be shared with one another.

We all can live life to the full. Every day of our lives, we can draw from a source of encouragement that will never fail. This source of strength we find in ourselves is **grace**, the gift of God's own life. We can lean on God without any fear of becoming too dependent. As we grow in God's life of grace, God is there to lead and support us each step of the way.

- What did Clare's classmates learn from her courage and spirit? How did they show courage and encouragement?

ACTIVITY

We all have challenges to overcome. Think of what stops you from living life fully every day. Create a reminder to yourself that every day is a gift of life to be shared with God and others.

Catholics Believe . . .

that the Holy Spirit helps us grow in grace as God's children.

Catechism, #1102

Scripture Story
The Son of God

God prepared the way for Jesus by sending John the Baptist. John was a **prophet**, someone called to speak God's message to humans. John preached and baptized people with water. He knew all along that someone greater was coming. John had been sent to baptize people so that when the greater one appeared, the people of Israel would know him.

John was baptizing people by the Jordan River when he saw Jesus walking toward him. John pointed Jesus out and called him the *Lamb of God*. He announced that Jesus was the one who was greater than he. Yet John still did not know that Jesus was the Son of God.

It was only when he baptized Jesus that John saw who Jesus was. During the baptism the Holy Spirit seemed to come down from the sky like a dove and rest upon Jesus. When John saw this sign, he knew that Jesus was the Son of God. He knew that Jesus was the one who would baptize with the Holy Spirit. Jesus would take away the sin of the world.

—based on John 1:25–34

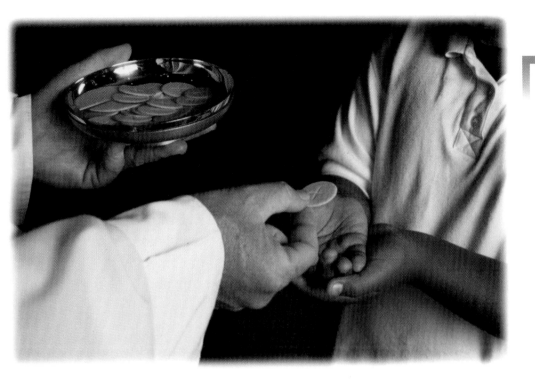

We meet God and share in God's grace through the sacraments, especially the Eucharist.

Children of God

Through the waters of Baptism, and through the power of the Holy Spirit, we become children of God. From the moment the waters of Baptism are poured on us, we are being **sanctified**, being made holy. To make sure that we continue to grow in this holiness, the Holy Spirit stands by us always. The Spirit is especially present to us in the **sacraments**, which are both signs and sources of grace. Sacraments are our celebrations of God's presence in our lives.

God chooses each one of us without any merit on our part. Being chosen by God without doing anything to deserve it may seem like a strange idea. Most of us value our freedom to choose and decide what to do in our lives. God's gift of grace cannot be earned. Grace is similar to the experience of another human choosing to love us without our doing anything about it or deserving it. God gives grace to us freely out of love for us. The gift of the Holy Spirit helps us trust completely in God's plan for us and cooperate with it.

Scripture Signpost

"For those who are led by the Spirit of God are children of God."

Romans 8:14

Who helps us become children of God?

The Work of the Spirit

We are not always ready to cooperate with God's plan. At times we think we are in charge of everything. No one can tell us what to do or how to do it. When we put ourselves at the center of our lives, the Spirit of God is squeezed into a small corner. When we think or act in a self-centered way, we do not allow ourselves to be led by the Holy Spirit.

Jesus invites us to open ourselves to the Spirit, to let the Spirit rush in and move us. The Holy Spirit is there without fail, even when we go wrong. God's Spirit leads us to pray even when it seems that words will not come. The Spirit shows us God's love even when we have turned away from it.

In truth, we are the unfinished work of the Spirit. God's Spirit helps us become a holy people. If we let the Spirit guide us, we become eager to do what is good. We continue to grow in holiness. As we do, we come to understand that God's life of grace in us is **immortal**. It is there in us without end. It is everlasting.

We are the work of the Spirit. How does the Holy Spirit help us become the people we are meant to be?

We cannot see God's Holy Spirit, though we can see the results of the Spirit's work. We have many symbolic ways to picture the Holy Spirit.

Symbols of the Holy Spirit

Symbol	Meaning
Water	The Spirit of God brings us new birth in the waters of Baptism.
Anointing	Anointing with oil shows a person is protected by God and set apart for special service.
Fire	Fire represents the Spirit's power to transform our lives.
Cloud and Light	God's Spirit led the Israelites as a pillar of cloud and light.
Hand	The hand is a sign of the Holy Spirit's power to heal and bless.
Dove	The dove suggests the presence of the Spirit as a sign of peace and gentleness.

RECALL

What is grace? Who helps us enjoy the special relationship we have with God through grace?

THINK AND SHARE

How do you think our daily lives would be different if we were more open to the Holy Spirit?

CONTINUE THE JOURNEY

God's grace is available throughout our journey of faith. On the map below, draw symbols for or write about three times in your life when you have experienced grace or felt the presence of the Holy Spirit.

FAITH MAP

BAPTISM

TO THE FUTURE

WE LIVE OUR FAITH

At Home   Find two ways to be a person of spirit for your family. Do something practical to bring joy, encouragement, and support to family members.

In the Parish   Talk with individuals who have recently celebrated the Sacrament of Confirmation. Ask them how they prepared to receive the Holy Spirit in this special way.

Come, Holy Spirit

The feast of **Pentecost,** 50 days after Easter, celebrates the gift of the Holy Spirit to the Church. On this day we recall how the Holy Spirit came upon the apostles in their gathering place. The Spirit turned frightened people into messengers on fire with good news (Acts 2:1–4). During the Mass on Pentecost, we sing a special song of praise in honor of the Holy Spirit, the one who makes us holy.

Pray together these words based on the Pentecost song.

PRAYER

Come, Holy Spirit, and shine your light on us!
Come, giver of God's gifts! Come, light of our
hearts!
Light most blessed, shine in the darkest hour,
for without you we can do nothing.
Open our hearts to God's love.
Open our lives to God's grace.
On our journey of faith, shine your light to show
us the way.

Review

Fill in the Blanks   Complete each sentence with the correct term.

1. The power that enables us to believe God is with us is

   called _____ .

2. In _____ we offer words and actions to God in public praise and thanks.

3. The official prayers and rites of the Church are known as

   the _____ .

4. The _____ is a day of worship and rest in honor of God.

5. The gift of God's own life is _____ .

Multiple Choice   Write the letter of the choice that best completes the sentence.

_____ 1. Jesus' closest and most trusted companions were the (a) Gospels
(b) apostles (c) poor (d) sick.

_____ 2. The Third Commandment reminds us that (a) we have a duty to
worship God (b) there is a time and place for individual acts of
worship (c) God loves us and believes in us (d) we must love
our families.

_____ 3. We receive the gift of faith (a) in the Sacrament of Baptism
(b) at the Mass (c) in the human touch (d) when we are suffering.

_____ 4. The greatest act of worship in the Catholic Church is (a) prayer
(b) the Rosary (c) the Eucharist (d) fasting.

_____ 5. To show his friends that they should serve one another, Jesus
(a) baptized them (b) healed them (c) washed their feet
(d) forgave them.

Share Your Faith   A good friend of yours who is not Catholic asks you the meaning of ordinary things such as water, bread, and wine in our worship. How would you explain the part such things play in worship among Catholics?

Show How Far You've Come

Use this chart to show what you have learned. For each chapter, write the three most important things you remember.

We Worship Our God

Chapter 5 We All Seek God	Chapter 6 In Prayer and Worship	Chapter 7 God in Us

What Else Would You Like to Know?

List any questions you still have about how we come to know and honor God.

_____

_____

_____

Continue the Journey

Choose one or more of the following activities to do on your own, with your class, or with your family.

- Look through your Faith Journal pages for Unit Two. Choose your favorite activity and share it with a friend or family member.

- Compose a brief prayer that gives thanks and praise to God for all the gifts you have received in your life.

- Take part in the Church's liturgy as a server, a reader, or a member of the choir. Prepare carefully for your part.

Called to Holiness

PRAYER

God, you make all saints holy by the power of your grace. Help us love you as your saints do now and forever.

On Halloween night the streets are full of ghosts and goblins, Western sheriffs and ballet dancers, kung fu masters and space aliens. We all have fun being something we're not.

As Catholics we celebrate the day after Halloween as the feast of who we *are* and who we want to become. November 1, the Feast of All Saints, is a time to celebrate mothers and husbands, kings and shoemakers, teachers and soldiers, and people next door. Saints are people who answered God's call to holiness with their lives, as we are called to do. The word **saint** means "holy one."

Don't make the mistake of thinking of saints as faraway fairy-tale characters, too perfect to imitate. All saints started out as ordinary people, gifted with God's grace as we were at Baptism. All saints lived in families, faced troubles, laughed at jokes, and loved fiercely. What sets the saints apart is what they did with their daily lives. Saints let the grace of God shine through every moment so they became living signs of God's love.

ACTIVITY

Design a Halloween costume that shows your true self—the person God is calling you to be.

Landmark The Church honors many saints with a formal process called **canonization**. This picture shows a canonization ceremony in Rome. Canonized saints are honored on their feast days. Many other saints have never been formally canonized. All Saints' Day is their feast day.

A Cloud of Witnesses

The Church honors saints in many ways. The more familiar saints have their own feast days in the Church's liturgical calendar. Parishes and schools are named for them. *People* are often named for saints, too. Your first or middle name may be that of a saint, your patron saint. Saints are chosen to be **patrons**, or special protectors and role models, of persons, countries, and organizations.

But not all saints are well known. We believe that every person, famous or hidden, simple or great, is called to sainthood. Anyone whose life touches others with God's love answers that call. On the first day of November, we honor the countless saints whose names only God remembers. We know that they have not forgotten us. They will stand with us as we grow, in holiness and love, into the people we are meant to be.

"Therefore, since we are surrounded by so great a cloud of witnesses, let us rid ourselves of every burden and sin that clings to us and persevere in running the race that lies before us, while keeping our eyes fixed on Jesus . . ."
—*Hebrews 12:1–2*

Catholics Believe . . .

that the saints are models for our own growth in holiness and love.

Catechism, #957

RECALL

What is canonization? When do we celebrate the saints who do not have special feast days?

THINK AND SHARE

Saints have been signs of God's love in thousands of different ways. How do you think saints living today might show God's love?

CONTINUE THE JOURNEY

Imagine you are honored as a saint in the future. Draw yourself in the Book of Saints. Fill out the information.

Book of Saints

Saint _____
(YOUR NAME)

of _____
(YOUR TOWN)

was best known for

_____
(HOW YOU SHOWED GOD'S LOVE)

_____

_____

_____

WE LIVE OUR FAITH

At Home Find out from your family if you have a patron saint for whom you were named. Or have your family help you choose a patron saint. Learn about your patron together.

In the Parish Participate in your parish's celebration of All Saints' Day.

There for Us

We adore and worship God alone. Yet by honoring the saints, we honor God. When we seek God's help in our prayers, we sometimes ask the saints to **intercede** for us, or take our prayers to God. Still, it is God alone who answers our prayers. God alone gives us everything that is good.

A **litany** is a series of short prayers with a repeated response. In the Litany of the Saints, we ask all the holy ones—known and unknown—to join their prayers with ours. Pray part of this litany together. If you wish, add the names of your patron saints to the list.

PRAYER

Holy Mary, Queen of All Saints, pray for us.
All you holy angels and archangels . . .
All you prophets and ancestors in faith . . .
All you apostles and disciples . . .
All you holy martyrs . . .
All you teachers and ministers . . .
All you holy men and women, saints of God, pray for us!

CHAPTER 9
The Image of God

PRAYER

God our Father, we see you in your Son, Jesus. Help us be signs of your love in our world.

It was a glorious morning. The sun was bright, and the blue sky was dotted with big, puffy clouds. A girl was waiting for the school bus with her father. Their conversation, inspired by the beautiful day, took an interesting turn.

Daughter: Wow! Look at the clouds.

Father: They're amazing—all different shapes. You can almost see things in them. I see horses galloping right there. See them?

Daughter: Sort of. Can we see God up there if we look really hard?

Father: Not exactly. God isn't visible the way horses and clouds are. I think we have to look for God differently.

Daughter: What do you mean?

What Does God Look Like?

It's not easy to imagine God. We see traces of God everywhere in the universe. From the glorious sun, moon, and stars in the heavens to the smallest creature on earth, each part of creation reflects the goodness of the Creator. But none of these things fully reveals who God is.

Our attempts to describe what God is like also fall short. When we call God "Father," for example, we might be imagining God as a father who loves and cares for a family. God does love and care for us. But God's "parental" love is much greater than that of the best parent we can imagine. God is far beyond the limits of our language and vision. No image or word we choose can capture who God is.

ACTIVITY

How would you describe God? Use words or pictures to show your image of God.

We Meet God in Jesus

We do not know what God looks like, but in Jesus we can see and hear God's love. The Gospel of John calls Jesus "the Word made flesh" *(John 1:14)*. For people in Jesus' time, words had great power. To call Jesus *God's Word* is to say that all the power and greatness of God has come to life in our midst.

In the mystery of the incarnation, the Son of God became human. The word **incarnation** means "coming into flesh." In Jesus, God became human to save us from sin. The Son of God came to show us the way to know, love, and serve God. He became one of us. From that moment on our lives were made holy. Eternal life became our destiny.

We call the incarnation a mystery because we can understand it only through faith. Through faith we can say that Jesus is both God and human. Jesus is the perfect image and sacrament of God. When we meet Jesus, we meet God.

Landmark Eastern Christians show their belief in Jesus' divinity by picturing him as a great ruler. Images like this one in a Greek church are titled *Christos Pantocrator,* "Christ, Lord of the Universe."

A Sign of Opposition

Gradually, in what he said and did, Jesus let people come to know God through him. Many people saw and heard and felt God's love in Jesus. Many others had difficulty accepting Jesus as the image of God. Not only during his life among us, but for centuries afterward, people have struggled to find a way to put their experience of Jesus into words.

Some could accept Jesus as human but not as **divine**, that is, God. Others had no difficulty believing that Jesus was divine but could not accept that Jesus was human. How is it possible for someone to be both divine and human?

When Jesus was a baby, Mary and Joseph presented him in the Temple. A holy man named Simeon predicted that Jesus was destined to be a sign of opposition (*Luke 2:25–35*). In other words, he would not be what people expected. Jesus would never be limited to easy categories because God's love is unlimited.

But the people Jesus touched and healed had no problem believing that he was both human and the Son of God. We share that same faith. We look at Jesus and we see God.

What are some ways Jesus showed God's love?

Scripture Signpost

"For God so loved the world that he gave his only Son, so that everyone who believes in him might not perish but might have eternal life."
John 3:16

What reason does the Gospel writer give for the incarnation?

ACTIVITY

Make a list of actions you can do at home and at school to show that you are living your baptismal call to be like Jesus.

Saints Walk with Us

Saint John of Damascus
Feast Day: March 27

Saint John of Damascus defended the practice of showing Jesus in pictures. He said that Jesus himself was a living *icon,* or image, of God.

Icons, or holy paintings, like this one were among the first images used in Christian churches.

God's Image in Us

We are created in God's image. But that image was blurred by the effects of original sin. The Sacrament of Baptism restores that image to its true beauty. In Baptism we are given the grace to be living images of God every day.

Of course we are not perfect images of God's love as Jesus is. But the image of God's love in us becomes clearer the more we try to live as Jesus did. The more we cooperate with God's grace, and the more we care for others, the more we reflect God's image.

People can see God at work even in our limited human selves. What we do and say reflects God's presence in the world around us. Like Jesus, we are sons and daughters of humanity. In Christ we are adopted sons and daughters of God. Through Baptism the mystery of the incarnation is our mystery, too, because we have been baptized into the life of Jesus.

● When people look for God's presence in our world, what signs will they see in us?

Images of Jesus

People of different cultures imagine Jesus differently. The great variety of images helps us understand that Jesus is truly the sacrament—the one great universal sign—of God's love.

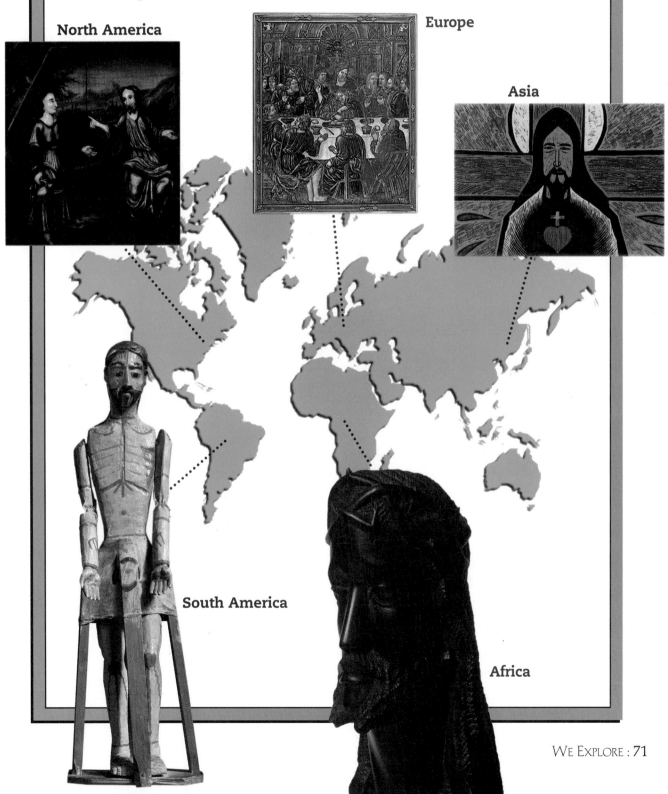

North America

Europe

Asia

South America

Africa

RECALL

What do we mean by the mystery of the incarnation? Why did the Son of God become human?

THINK AND SHARE

Why is it important to remember that what we say and do can reflect God's love?

CONTINUE THE JOURNEY

Imagine that you have just heard Jesus teach or shared a meal with him or been healed by him. Write a letter to a friend describing your experience. Tell what you learned about God from being with Jesus.

WE LIVE OUR FAITH

At Home   With family members, look for images of Jesus at home or in library art books. Choose your favorite image and share your reasons for choosing it.

In the Parish   Find out what ethnic groups are represented in your parish. Talk with a parishioner from an ethnic group other than your own about how Jesus is pictured in his or her culture.

Shine Through Us, Lord

Words on a page and pictures in a frame, no matter how beautiful, will never fully capture God's love. That love is a living thing, and it can be seen for what it really is only in action.

The words and images we use in prayer are good and beautiful. And we can make our *lives* a prayer, too. In our loving actions, people will see Jesus. They will see God's love.

Prayer

Think of one way you can make your life a prayer. Make the Sign of the Cross with holy water as a reminder of your Baptism. Then pray together for help in carrying out your action.

Lord Jesus,
help us spread your love everywhere.
Shine through us, and be so much in us
that everyone with whom we come in contact
may feel your presence within us.
Let them look at us
and in us
see you.

—*based on a prayer of Cardinal Newman*

CHAPTER 10

Stories and Signs

PRAYER

God of love and power, open our hearts so that we may recognize your kingdom. Teach us to find our own stories in Jesus' parables.

Once there was a very rich man who gave his only son everything he wanted. When the young man took over his father's business, he threw his father out like an old shoe. Abandoned, the old man wept and wandered in the streets.

Some years later the selfish son had a son of his own. One bitterly cold day the old man returned and met his grandson outside the house. "Please get me a blanket to keep me warm," the old man begged. The young boy ran into the house and up to the attic. He found a thick wool blanket and began tearing it in two. The boy's father heard the noise. "Why are you tearing that blanket?" the annoyed father asked. The youngster replied, "I am going to give one piece to my grandfather now, and I am going to save the other half for you when you are old."

We've all heard stories we will always remember. Perhaps a surprise ending caught us off guard or made us look at the world in a different way. In stories frogs turn into princes. Children outsmart powerful villains. We soar on the backs of dragons or with the wings of eagles. These unlikely events remind us that things are not always as they appear. Stories have the power to lead us into different worlds—worlds of enchantment and wonder.

Jesus, too, has stories for us. They are also invitations to another world. Some of Jesus' stories are like windows that allow us to see God. Others are like mirrors that show us something about ourselves. Try to listen to Jesus' stories with a sense of wonder and imagination. Let yourself be surprised by God's word.

Why do people of all ages like listening to stories? Why do people like telling stories?

God's Kingdom Is Here!

Everywhere he went, Jesus invited people to enter the kingdom of God. The **kingdom of God** is not an earthly place or government. It is God's reign of peace and justice. Jesus used *signs*—actions and examples—and stories to teach about God's reign.

Jesus showed people that there are reminders of God's kingdom in creation. The signs in creation say that God is near and God is great. Jesus worked mighty deeds called **miracles** as physical signs of God's power. He healed the sick and forgave sinners. He did these things, not to show off his own power, but to be a living sign of God's love.

After a while, however, the crowds demanded miracle upon miracle, expecting Jesus to perform as if he were a magician. But Jesus' miracles were not magic acts performed to trick people into believing. Jesus told the crowds they had it backward. The believing comes first and is most important. When we believe and trust in God, we recognize that anything is possible.

Luke 10:29–37

Matthew 13:44

Catholics Believe . . .

that Jesus used stories and signs to teach us about the kingdom of God.

Catechism, #546–547

ACTIVITY

Choose one of the parables pictured. Read the story in your Bible. Then tell it to a classmate in your own words.

Matthew 25:1–13

Luke 15:8–10

What Is This Kingdom of God Like?

Jesus' words were as powerful as his signs. When he spoke, he spoke from the heart. To teach people about the kingdom of God, Jesus used simple but memorable stories that had special meaning for his listeners. We call these stories **parables**.

With each parable he told, Jesus invited his listeners to use their own experiences to imagine what the kingdom of God was like. For example, Jesus told laborers working the land that the kingdom of heaven was like a treasure hidden in a field. To a poor woman down to her last small coin, Jesus said the kingdom of God was like a lost coin found again.

Jesus insisted that people listen with their hearts as well as their ears to what God was asking of them in the stories he told. The parables show that to enter the kingdom of God, a person might have to give up many things the world considers important. Wealth, power, and fashion don't count in God's kingdom. The treasures of God's kingdom are love, justice, and peace.

Through his stories and signs, Jesus showed us that God's kingdom is not a faraway fairy tale. It is here in our midst. When we love, when we act justly, when we make peace, we are living in the reign of God.

Scripture Signpost

"Many began to believe in his name when they saw the signs he was doing."

John 2:23

Where do you think people today can look for signs of God's love?

We Belong to the Kingdom

Our Moral Guide

Living in the kingdom of God involves making wise choices and acting justly. We enter into God's reign by admitting that we need God's help to do what is asked of us.

Catechism, #1431

Why do you think people find it difficult to turn to God?

In Baptism we are given new life. We are invited to keep turning to God with heart, mind, and soul. We did nothing to deserve this gift and invitation. We are like the widow whom Jesus saw weeping at the death of her only son. Moved with pity, Jesus stopped the funeral procession. He touched the dead young man, brought him to life, and gave him to the care of his mother (*Luke 7:11–17*). Even more importantly, God gives us the great gift of eternal life. We become citizens of God's kingdom.

The kingdom is already in our midst, like a seed sprouting, but it has yet to come in fullness. At every Eucharist we pray the Lord's Prayer and repeat the words "your kingdom come." While waiting for the kingdom to come in fullness, we need to be aware that we can miss its presence in our midst.

Jesus called people to *repent*, which literally means to "think again," "to make a better choice." **Repentance** means turning away from sin and turning toward God. Repentance helps us see the kingdom of God more clearly. When we take care to choose the just and loving way, we are living in the kingdom of God.

How can we show that the kingdom of God is already in our midst?

Understanding a Parable

To understand the parables Jesus told, we need to think differently. When we read or hear parables in Scripture, it helps to be aware of certain features that parables have in common.

Here are some clues to follow:

- Watch for a question that may trigger a parable, such as "Who is my neighbor?" or "How often must I forgive my brother?" Note that Jesus may answer the question that invites the parable with another question at the end of the parable.

- Look or listen for the words "The kingdom of heaven is like," which usually lead off a parable.

- Note that the setting and characters of a parable are usually taken from everyday life. For example, in a parable you might encounter people baking, farming, or caring for animals.

- Observe that characters in a parable sometimes do not act in ways individuals would act in real life. Take, for instance, the father who gives his son his entire inheritance, the master who serves his servant, or the king who puts up with insults from his subjects.

- Be prepared for surprise endings that appear to be "unfair" in the eyes of the world. These surprise endings make us think twice about what God is really asking of us.

Where Will This Lead Me?

Following these steps will help you recognize parables in Jesus' teaching and better understand their meaning as invitations to the kingdom of God.

RECALL

What is a parable? What is a miracle?

THINK AND SHARE

In what ways is the Sacrament of Baptism like a miracle?

CONTINUE THE JOURNEY

Write your own parable. Think of a message that people today need to hear about God's kingdom. Use what you know about parables to put your message in story form.

A Parable for Today

WE LIVE OUR FAITH

At Home   Plan a family storytelling time. Share family members' favorite stories. Include your favorite parable or miracle story.

In the Parish   Identify people in your faith community who are public signs of God's kingdom. Write thank-you notes to or create awards for these "Miracle Workers."

Working Miracles

All around the world, people point the way to God's kingdom with words and with actions. These people make a difference in the world. They work miracles every day in quiet but powerful ways.

We support these miracle workers by contributing our talents or our money or our time. We learn from their example. And we support them with our prayers.

PRAYER

Take turns telling about someone you know, or someone you have read about or heard about, who is working to make a difference in the world. After each person shares a story, respond by praying together: "Yours is the kingdom, the power, and the glory, now and for ever."

CHAPTER 11

The Way to New Life

PRAYER

Jesus, our Savior and Brother, you chose to live our life and die our death. Show us the way to new life through the sacraments.

How do you feel when a friend betrays you or when someone you love is in pain? No one likes to suffer or see others suffer needlessly. Yet experience soon teaches us that suffering is woven into the pattern of our lives. Suffering and death are part of the human condition. They are some of the effects of original sin.

The mysteries of suffering and death are part of life. We can choose how we look at these mysteries. We can let them teach us. Too often, though, we don't face these realities at all. We turn away from suffering and death, our own and that of others. We pretend they don't exist.

ACTIVITY

List some examples of ways we try to avoid or ignore suffering and death.

Images of Mary holding her son's body are not based on Scripture, but they express the great sadness of human suffering and death. The traditional name for these images is *Pietà*, from the Italian word for "pity" or "compassion."

We have an example of suffering and death turned upside down in Jesus. Jesus' answer to the mystery of suffering and death was not to turn away but to enter into it. By his great **compassion**, or willingness to suffer as others do, Jesus showed us the way through suffering and beyond death to eternal life.

Jesus could have avoided the effects of sin. He chose instead to experience them, out of love for sinners. Jesus chose to go through betrayal and denial by his friends. He was tried, tortured, and executed. He did not choose these things because he liked pain and suffering. Jesus walked the way of suffering and death to save us. He wants us to trust him enough to follow him into new life.

The Son of God accepted his suffering as God's will, and so he is our **redeemer**. He is the one who saves us from sin and everlasting death.

Scripture Signpost

"We were indeed buried with him through baptism into death, so that, just as Christ was raised from the dead by the glory of the Father, we too might live in newness of life."
Romans 6:4

What is the connection between Jesus' death and resurrection and the Sacrament of Baptism?

Catholics Believe . . .

that we share in the mystery of Jesus' life, death, and resurrection through the sacraments.

Catechism, #1115

SCRIPTURE STORY

In the Name of Jesus Christ

The man waited outside the Temple gate, the gate called Beautiful, as he had waited every day he could remember. For 40 years he had waited, lying there in the dust where his relatives left him each morning. By his side a clay bowl waited, too, for the jingle of coins.

The waiting man was a beggar born with a body so twisted he could not sit or stand or walk. He could not even raise a hand to shield his eyes from the glare of the late afternoon sun.

Then shadows fell across his face—two men on their way to the Temple for prayer. The beggar moved his lips painfully. "A coin or two?" he asked. "Anything, for the love of God?"

The two men stared down at him. Their eyes did not carry the impatience or pity or fear that the beggar was used to. There was nothing in these eyes but compassion. The beggar stared back, hungry and hopeful.

ACTIVITY

Tell a story or draw a picture about a time when you experienced "new life" after a time of waiting or difficulty.

One of the men spoke. "We have neither silver nor gold," he said. "But what we have we will gladly share. In the name of Jesus Christ, rise and walk!"

The man who had spoken took the astonished beggar by the right hand. His companion leaned over to take the left. In front of a crowd of startled onlookers, three men passed through the Beautiful Gate that afternoon to praise God. It was later noted that the third man—the one in the middle, the one who had been waiting 40 years—did not limit his prayers to words. He danced his joy with his whole body, as full of delight as a newborn child.

—based on Acts 3:1–10

Signs of New Life

The story of the cure of the beggar by the Beautiful Gate is not about a miracle performed by Jesus. The two men in the story are the apostles Peter and John, two of Jesus' closest followers. They had lived through the terrible time of Jesus' arrest, trial, and crucifixion. They had been witnesses to his **resurrection**, or rising to new life, the triumph over death brought about by God's great power. They had seen Jesus return to his heavenly Father. And they had known the fire of the Holy Spirit coming into their lives. But their work was just beginning. They had been sent to the world with a message of good news: sin and death are not the end.

- **What do you think the work of Jesus' followers was? How can we do this work?**

Jesus Is the Way

When Jesus walked the path of suffering and death to the new life of God's kingdom, he did so as the first of many. "I am the way," he told his followers. "Whoever believes in me will do the works that I do" *(John 14:6,12)*.

The followers of Jesus watched closely and did as he had done. They called people to repentance and baptized them in water, as Jesus had told them to do. They called upon the power of the Holy Spirit to transform hearts as their own had been transformed at Pentecost. In the name of Jesus, they forgave sin and cured illness. They celebrated the miracle of Christian love as Jesus had done at the wedding feast in Cana. And they laid hands on a new generation, commissioning them to carry on the work.

In each of these ways, the followers of Jesus proclaimed the message of God's reign. Suffering, sin, and death do not win. God's power and love break through into our lives. New life comes through Jesus.

We are Jesus' followers today, and we still do the works that he does. We proclaim the same message. We celebrate the mystery of Jesus' life, death, and resurrection. We call this the **Paschal mystery**, from the Hebrew word for *Passover*, because Jesus "passed over" from death to new life to save us.

Our Moral Guide

The *Works of Mercy* are acts of compassion and charity that we do for our neighbors. Through these actions we participate in the Paschal mystery.

Catechism, #2447

Why is it important to show compassion for people's physical needs as well as for their spiritual needs?

What does this picture show? What actions of Jesus does this sacrament remind us of?

The Paschal Mystery

Each of the sacraments celebrates, in some way, the Paschal mystery of Jesus' dying and rising to new life. Each offers us a new way of looking at the mystery of our own lives. Jesus, who died and rose, is at work in and through the sacraments.

Confirmation

We die to selfishness and live in compassion as the Holy Spirit moves us to acts of charity and service.

Baptism

We die with Christ in the waters of Baptism and then rise up to the new life of grace.

Eucharist

This sacrificial meal is our greatest celebration of the Paschal mystery. In the Eucharist we enter into Jesus' saving death and resurrection. We rise and go forth to serve God as Jesus did.

Holy Orders

We die to our own will and rise to a new life of ordained ministry to God's people.

Matrimony

We die to ourselves and become one with another, rising to new life in a family.

Reconciliation

We die to sin and rise to new life in forgiveness and community.

Anointing of the Sick

We become one with Jesus' suffering and death and rise to renewed health or pass over to eternal life.

RECALL

What name do we give to the mystery of Jesus' suffering, death, and resurrection? How do we celebrate that mystery today?

THINK AND SHARE

How do you think life would be different if we did not have Jesus' example to follow?

CONTINUE THE JOURNEY

Make a diptych—a two-part picture. On the left, draw an action of Jesus that shows his compassion. On the right, draw a similar action of Jesus' followers today.

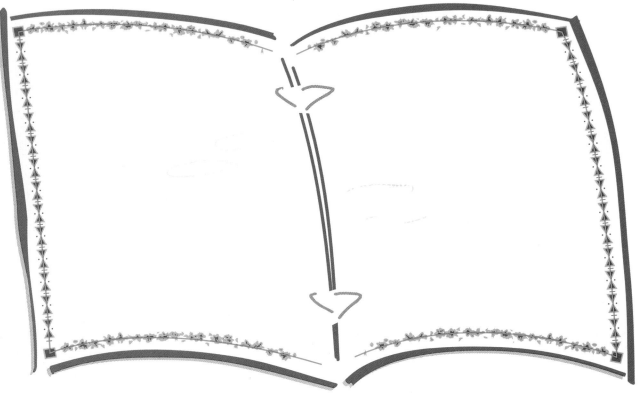

WE LIVE OUR FAITH

At Home Choose one of the Works of Mercy (page 223). Show compassion to a family member in this way.

In the Parish As a class or with a partner, volunteer to do chores for a parishioner who is hospitalized or housebound. Remember this person in your prayers, too.

Lord, Have Mercy

Praying for the sick and for those who have died is a work of mercy. Show your compassion by praying the following *litany*, or prayer of petition, together. This litany may be used during funeral liturgies. After each petition, respond, "Lord, have mercy."

PRAYER

Risen Lord, pattern of our life forever . . .
Promise and image of what we shall be . . .
Son of God who came to destroy sin
  and death . . .
Word of God who delivered us from the
  fear of death . . .
Crucified Lord, forsaken in death, raised
  in glory . . .
Lord Jesus, gentle Shepherd who brings
  rest to our souls . . .
Lord Jesus, you bless those who mourn
  and are in pain. Bless us, too, we pray . . .

—from the Order of Christian Funerals

Review

Matching
Match the meanings in Column A with the correct terms in Column B.

Column A

_b_ 1. Turn away from sin and turn toward God.

_d_ 2. Story Jesus told about the kingdom of God.

_e_ 3. Mighty deed done by Jesus.

_c_ 4. The mystery of God's Son becoming human to save us.

_a_ 5. Jesus' suffering, death, and resurrection.

Column B

a. incarnation

b. repent

c. Paschal mystery

d. parable

e. miracle

Complete the Sentence
Circle the term that will complete each sentence correctly.

1. We are made in the (image, incarnation) of God.

2. Jesus invites (everyone, only saints) to enter the kingdom of God.

3. The sacraments celebrate the (parable, Paschal) mystery.

4. The Sacrament of (Anointing of the Sick, Baptism) begins our new life in Christ.

5. The apostles Peter and (John, Paul) healed a man outside the Beautiful Gate of the Temple.

Share Your Faith
A friend asks why the sacraments are so important to Catholics. What do you tell your friend?

Show How Far You've Come

Use this chart to show what you have learned. For each chapter, write or draw the three most important things you remember.

Jesus Is a Sacrament		
Chapter 9 *The Image of God*	**Chapter 10** *Stories and Signs*	**Chapter 11** *The Way to New Life*

What Else Would You Like to Know?

List any questions you still have about Jesus as a sacrament—a living sign and experience of God's love.

_____

_____

_____

Continue the Journey

Choose one or more of the following activities to do on your own, with your class, or with your family.

- Look through your Faith Journal pages for Unit Three. Choose your favorite activity and share it with a friend or family member.

- Make a scrapbook of the Works of Mercy as they are performed today. From magazines and newspapers, clip articles and photographs about such actions performed in your community, in the rest of the country, and around the world.

- Choose one of the Gospels and read through it, reading a little each day. Keep a list of questions you have about what you read. Share these with a family member, a classmate, or your teacher. Look for answers together.

Waiting for the Light

PRAYER

God of times and seasons, in a joyful spirit we celebrate the coming of Jesus, the Light of the World. Help us prepare for his coming again in glory.

Imagine a night so dark you can't see even faint shapes. Imagine a time so cold that your breath freezes into a snowy cloud. It seems as if the sun went down days ago and it will be months until it rises again. Or maybe it won't rise at all!

Thousands of years ago, people didn't need to imagine what a cold nighttime world would be like. Without electric lights or central heating, winter seemed endless. People grew afraid. Their fear was strongest around the *winter solstice*, the day with the fewest hours of light.

During that longest night, people prayed and sang and sacrificed, begging the sun to rise again.

And it did. Day by day, the light grew stronger, warming the earth and stirring the life-giving crops. It's no wonder that ancient people saw the sun as a powerful god and celebrated its yearly return.

It's no wonder that, as Christianity spread, people in the Northern Hemisphere associated the return of the sun after the winter solstice with the coming of Christ, the Light of the World. Soon people began celebrating the birthday of the Son of God in December, around the time they had once celebrated the birthday of the sun.

This painting illustrates Jesus' words in Revelation 3:20. Why do we call Jesus "the Light of the World"?

A Time of Preparation

The darkness of winter is not bad. Day and night, sun and moon are all God's creation. During the winter the earth rests and prepares itself for a new cycle of growth. In a similar way, we use the days of **Advent**, the four weeks leading up to Christmas, to prepare ourselves for the coming of Jesus.

We gather, as people always have, to pray and sing, share stories, and make sacrifices. We listen to the Scripture readings from the prophets. The prophets reminded God's people to prepare for the coming of the **Messiah**, God's chosen one, by living as people of light. We prepare our hearts, through the Sacrament of Reconciliation, to grow in love. We light candles on the Advent wreath. Each flame is a reminder of the light no darkness can put out.

RECALL

Why did celebrating Jesus' birth in December make sense to people of the Northern Hemisphere?

THINK AND SHARE

In our time, when people often begin celebrating Christmas on the day after Thanksgiving, how can we make Advent a time of prayerful preparation?

CONTINUE THE JOURNEY

On each of the sun's rays, write an example of someone or some situation in your world that needs light. In the center of the sun, write one way you can bring light this Advent.

WE LIVE OUR FAITH

At Home   Each week of Advent, do something together as a family to prepare yourselves and your world for the coming of Jesus.

In the Parish   Participate in an Advent Reconciliation service at your parish or another Catholic church.

Come, Lord Jesus

The **Advent wreath** is a circle of evergreen branches set with four candles. It is a glowing presence in our worship during the Season of Advent. The wreath is blessed during Mass. The entire assembly responds with the words "Come, Lord Jesus." These words proclaim our belief that Christ came first in the flesh and will come again in glory as the Risen One. The prayer that follows says that the light of each candle reflects the splendor of Christ's light. One candle is lighted for each Advent week.

Advent wreaths are often displayed in homes, too. The Advent wreath makes a good centerpiece for family meals, reminding us that we are growing in love.

PRAYER

Gather around the Advent wreath in your parish church or classroom. Pray together this ancient Advent prayer:

> **O Radiant Dawn,**
> **splendor of eternal light, sun of justice:**
> **come, shine on those who dwell in**
> **darkness**
> **and the shadow of death.**

CHAPTER 13

A Sign to the World

PRAYER

Light of the World, let us carry your love and your message to the ends of the earth.

"I want you to meet the archbishop," the priest said as soon as I got off the plane. I already felt uncomfortable in the heat, and the priest's invitation made me even more uncomfortable. I had never met a bishop, let alone an archbishop. All I could manage to say in response was, "That sounds great."

When we arrived at the archbishop's residence, the priest ushered me in the door and told me to make myself at home. He had to go upstairs for a few minutes, so I wandered into the living room and then into the kitchen. A man in a short-sleeved shirt was preparing dinner at the stove. He smiled and nodded hello to me. I nodded back. Then I went back to the living room and sat down. By the time the priest returned, I had run through all my ideas about what I would do and say when I met the archbishop.

"Come on, I'll introduce you to the archbishop," the priest said. I followed him into the kitchen, where he stopped by the cook at the stove.

"Tom, I would like to introduce Archbishop Berry."

"Glad to meet you, Tom," said the archbishop, shaking my hand. "How do you like your steak?"

Signs of Welcome

A warm smile and a welcoming handshake can go a long way toward making people feel at home. The way Archbishop Berry welcomed him made Tom feel comfortable in an unfamiliar situation. Archbishop Berry showed *hospitality*, the gift of caring for the needs of a guest. Tom learned a lot about Archbishop Berry by watching how he behaved.

As members of the Church, we are like Archbishop Berry. We have been sent to invite people into the reign of God and to help them feel at home there. We have a ministry of hospitality to the whole world. People will learn about us and about God's kingdom by watching how we behave.

Scripture Signpost

But you are "a chosen race, a royal priesthood, a holy nation, a people of his own, so that you may announce the praises" of him who called you out of darkness into his wonderful light.
1 Peter 2:9

According to this New Testament letter, what is the reason for the Church's existence?

ACTIVITY

Create several thought balloons that describe the thoughts and feelings of these young people as they complete their initiation into the Church.

What Is the Church?

The Church is not God's reign. But as the Church we point people *toward* God's reign. We are signs of God's kingdom. The whole world should be able to see God's love and power in action when they see the way we live as Church.

Through the Holy Spirit, Christ makes the Church one, holy, catholic, and apostolic. These are the identifying **marks of the Church**. They are the Church's signs by which all people can recognize and feel at home in God's kingdom.

In the Creed we recite the marks of the Church. The words are familiar. But do we know what they really mean? Sometimes it helps to take a new look at something familiar. Let's think about the Church as apostolic, catholic, holy, and one.

SCRIPTURE STORY

What special role in the Church do you think Jesus gave Peter?

Built upon the Apostles

When Jesus traveled into the region of Caesarea Philippi, he asked the apostles, "Who do people say the Son of Man is?" The apostles gave the usual answers: John the Baptist, Elijah, Jeremiah, or one of the other prophets.

Jesus was not satisfied with these familiar answers, so he asked the question again in a different form. "Who do *you* say that I am?" he asked. The apostle Peter made a quick reply to the new question, "You are the Messiah, the Son of the living God."

Jesus knew that only God could have shown Peter this. "And so," Jesus replied, "I say to you, you are Peter, and upon this rock I will build my church." Jesus also promised Peter the keys to the kingdom of heaven.

—based on Matthew 16:13–19

With these words Jesus entrusted his ministry to Peter and the other apostles. In a way he made them the foundation stones of the Church. By giving Peter the authority symbolized by keys, Jesus also showed that the Church and the kingdom of God are connected.

Jesus sent the apostles out to spread the good news of God's kingdom. The Church is **apostolic** because it was built on the apostles' efforts.

Opening the Door of Faith

The Spirit of Christ, the Holy Spirit, moved the apostles to spread the good news. Even so, building the Church was not easy. As the young community of faith grew, followers of Christ were persecuted for their beliefs.

A man named Saul of Tarsus, for example, set out to destroy Christ's followers. Saul believed they should be punished. But after he experienced the risen Jesus, his heart was changed. Then Saul was led by the Spirit to travel far and wide to spread the good news of salvation in Christ. Saul is known to us as Paul the Apostle.

Paul's own experience had taught him that all are welcome in the Church. Paul preached, "There is neither Jew nor Greek, there is neither slave nor free person, there is not male and female; for you are all one in Christ Jesus" *(Galatians 3:28)*. Paul taught that the Church was **catholic**, or universal. It has a mission to the whole human race. Paul understood what Jesus meant when he told the apostles to make *disciples,* or followers, of all nations *(Matthew 28:19)*. Jesus meant all people, not just some.

ACTIVITY

Make a list of ways we can share in Paul's mission to bring many kinds of people into the community of the Church.

A Holy and United People

Just as the Church was both apostolic and catholic from its beginnings, it was also holy and one. The Church is holy through Christ. Christ loved the Church and gave himself up to sanctify it. Christ also gave the Church the gift of the Holy Spirit. Through the power of the Holy Spirit, the members of the Church become *holy*, more closely resembling the image of God. We share in Christ's holiness through the waters of Baptism.

The Holy Spirit also leads the Church toward *unity*, or oneness. The Church believes in one Lord, shares one faith and one Baptism, forms one Body, and is given life by the one Spirit. The Spirit brings together all the faithful. In the gathering are many kinds of people, people of all backgrounds and ways of life. These different people come together as one people of God, one Church.

Teaching Authority

The Church is a community of faith. Our message needs to be *authentic,* or faithful to the truth, if we are to share that faith with others. When it comes to what the Church teaches, we turn to those who are best able to keep the Church faithful to the word of God. We turn to the magisterium—the pope and the bishops. The word **magisterium** means "teaching authority." With the guidance of the Holy Spirit, the magisterium protects and explains the word of God. It is not possible for the Holy Spirit to guide us in the wrong direction. Therefore we say that some of the Church's teachings are **infallible**, or free from error. Guided by the Spirit, the Church's leaders can help us settle questions of faith. They can deepen our understanding of the teachings of Jesus and the apostles.

Landmark The leaders of the Church sometimes gather for meetings called *councils.* They publish documents that explain the gospel message and the Church's teachings. This picture shows the opening of the Second Vatican Council (1962–1965), which helped the Church communicate its message to the modern world.

Images of the Church

The marks of the Church are not the only ways to describe our community of faith. The chart below shows some other important images of the Church.

People of God

The Church is a gathering of people who have been shaped by God. God's people are bound together by faith in God's promises. All are called to become people of God.

Body of Christ

The Church is a body or group of real people. The Church is one body in Christ, visible and spiritual, human and divine. Christ is the Head of the Body. The members of the Body of Christ are many but are united in one Church.

Pilgrim People

Pilgrims are people who travel together on a prayerful journey to a holy place. The Church is a pilgrim people journeying to its true home—eternal life with God.

Bride

The Church is the Bride of Christ. Christ loved the Church. He gave himself up for it and remains with it.

Teacher

Through its doctrine, life, and worship, the Church is a teacher like Jesus. The teaching authority of the Church, the pope and the bishops, leads the faithful of every generation by word and example.

Temple of the Holy Spirit

The Holy Spirit is the source of the Church's life. God's Spirit makes the Church a temple of holiness, a place where God lives. The Spirit leads members of the Church in prayer and worship and helps them develop their special gifts.

RECALL

What are the identifying marks of the Church? How is the Church apostolic?

THINK AND SHARE

How can the Church be described as catholic, or universal, when many people in the world do not belong to it?

CONTINUE THE JOURNEY

Draw a picture of the Church that illustrates one of its identifying marks as described in the Creed: one, holy, catholic, apostolic.

WE LIVE OUR FAITH

At Home Your family is a Church community. How does your family show unity, holiness, openness to all people, and faithfulness to the gospel message?

In the Parish Ask a parish staff member to help you find out how your parish is related to the greater local Church and its bishop. Investigate how parish pastors are appointed and what their responsibilities are.

To Be One in Christ

Each year in late January, Catholics and other Christians throughout the United States celebrate the Week of Prayer for Christian Unity. This annual celebration reminds us that we are not yet fully one. As Catholics we are called to reach out not only to other Christians but to all people. We still have work to do.

PRAYER

Almighty and eternal God,
you gather the scattered sheep
and watch over those you have gathered.
Look kindly on all who follow Jesus, your Son.
You have marked them with the seal of
   one Baptism,
now make them one in the fullness of faith
and unite them in the bond of love.
We ask this through Christ our Lord.
Amen.

CHAPTER 14

Steps on Our Journey

PRAYER

God of welcome, you wash us, anoint us, and feed us in Christ's sacraments. We thank you for giving us new life that lasts forever.

How do you measure change and growth? You can look at pencil marks on a doorway that measure how much you've grown. You can look back over old photograph albums. You can remember moving from one house or one town or one country to another. You can recall the first day of class in every grade.

Change and growth are natural parts of life. But that does not mean they happen easily. Often we are curious about ways in which our lives might be different or about new paths we might take. Taking the first step can be hard. Sometimes we hesitate. We may even take a step back and ask questions such as "What am I getting into?" and "What am I leaving behind?" Then, when we go forward, we must follow through.

There are many steps on our journey of faith. Baptism, our first step into the life of Christ, was easy for most of us. Our parents took that step for us. Our **godparents**, who were also there, promised to guide us in our growth as Catholics. As we grow in the life of Christ, we continue to take steps on our journey of faith.

ACTIVITY

Make a list of people who have helped you on your journey of faith.

SCRIPTURE STORY
Entering a New Life

How do you think Nicodemus reacted to what Jesus said?

One night a religious leader named Nicodemus came to see Jesus. He had heard that Jesus was a teacher from God. Jesus talked with Nicodemus about the kingdom of God. He told Nicodemus that a person has to be reborn to enter God's kingdom. A puzzled look came across Nicodemus's face. "How can someone be born again?" he wondered aloud. Jesus continued, "I tell you plainly. No one can enter the kingdom of God without being born of water and the Spirit." Nicodemus still did not understand and asked how it could happen.

Patiently Jesus explained God's plan to save all people. He told Nicodemus that God so loved the world he sent his only Son to bring everyone to eternal life. To enter into this new life, a person has to believe in God's only Son and be baptized in water and the Spirit. Once a person believes and is baptized, that person lives in the light.

That person knows the truth that Jesus is the Savior of the world.

—*based on John 3:1–21*

Scripture Signpost

"Amen, amen, I say to you, no one can enter the kingdom of God without being born of water and Spirit."

John 3:5

What did Jesus mean by "born of water and Spirit"?

● **How would you explain Jesus' answer to Nicodemus in your own words?**

Why is it not possible to become a member of the Church just by taking a test?

One Step at a Time

Jenny had wanted to take this step for many years. Although she was twenty-three years old, she could feel butterflies in her stomach. She rang the doorbell of St. Benedict's and asked to see the pastor. As soon as Father Paul sat down with her, Jenny blurted out, "I want to be baptized. I want to become a Catholic. What tests do I have to take?" The priest smiled warmly and said, "Let's take one step at a time. Becoming a Catholic means continuing your journey of faith. Members of the community of the Church will help you on your way. The process of becoming a member of the Church, what we call **initiation**, takes time."

The idea that it would take some time to enter the Church puzzled Jenny. "But I thought," she began, trying to express her jumbled thoughts and feelings, "that all you had to do was memorize answers to some questions and you could be baptized." Again the priest smiled. He invited Jenny to a gathering the next night. He explained that a group of others like herself were going to meet at a parishioner's home. "There you'll meet people who are on similar journeys. You can share stories with each other and begin to listen to the story of salvation."

The Journey Continues

After several months of asking questions and listening to the stories of the gospel, Jenny entered the **catechumenate**. During this period of growing in faith, she was never alone in her journey. At every step the community walked with her. They shared the Scriptures with her, discussing the meaning of God's word.

Jenny also had support from her **sponsor**, Ellen. Ellen's job was to be a companion to Jenny on her journey. Ellen was there to help show Jenny the way. Jenny could also count on others in the catechumenate and on many of the parishioners to be there for her. Their lives were an example to her. From their example Jenny came to know and love the Christian way of life.

ACTIVITY

Select a story of faith you have learned this year that you find meaningful. Retell the story to a partner and explain what it means to you.

A Night to Remember

It had been almost eighteen months since Jenny had first spoken with Father Paul. In that time Jenny had drawn closer to her new community. Since the First Sunday of Lent, she had become one of the **elect**, or "chosen." She had been chosen by the Church to move toward full initiation, or membership.

Conversion is a lifelong process of turning to God. The process begins with Baptism, but it does not end there. We are often tempted to turn away from God and choose what we want. This tendency to turn away is called **concupiscence**. It is one of the effects of original sin.

Catechism, #1426

How do we fight temptation and keep ourselves focused on conversion?

Jenny was going to be fully initiated into the Church that night at the Easter Vigil. She would receive the Sacraments of Initiation—Baptism, Confirmation, and Eucharist. At the baptismal pool, Father Paul asked Jenny to declare her faith in God the Father, Son, and Holy Spirit. Then Jenny stepped into the pool. As Father Paul *immersed* her in the water, he prayed, "I baptize you in the name of the Father." He repeated the action two more times, in the names of the Son and of the Holy Spirit. Through her Baptism Jenny experienced a rebirth in Christ. In him she experienced forgiveness of sin and was made holy. Her spirit was renewed. She was a changed person, destined for eternal life with God.

ACTIVITY

The Church welcomes people of all ages as members. Ask five members of your parish when they were initiated.

A little later Jenny and the others who had just been baptized came into the church wearing white garments and carrying lighted candles. The parishioners applauded, and Father Paul greeted the newly baptized at the altar. After a brief prayer Father Paul placed his hands on each of those to be confirmed. When he anointed Jenny with the **chrism**, or holy oil, he prayed, "Jenny, be sealed with the Gift of the Holy Spirit." She responded, "Amen."

Finally, the moment came to receive the Eucharist. Jenny stood before Father Paul to receive the host and the cup. "The Body of Christ, the Blood of Christ" echoed in her mind and heart. Jenny's "Amen" meant that she believed she was receiving the Body and Blood of Christ.

Only the Beginning

Like Jenny, each one of us is changed by becoming a Christian. Whether we are baptized as infants or later in life, a new way of life begins for us at Baptism. The Sacraments of Confirmation and Eucharist complete our initiation as members of the Church. With these sacraments the Church welcomes, accepts, and initiates each of us into Christ. The Sacraments of Initiation do not mark the end of our journey of faith. They are only the beginning.

As our journey continues, we take time to renew the promises made at Baptism.

RECALL

What is initiation? What are the three Sacraments of Initiation?

THINK AND SHARE

What do you think a person baptized as an infant can learn from someone who was initiated into the Church later in life?

CONTINUE THE JOURNEY

Write a thank-you note to your godparents or to someone in your parish community for helping you take a step on your journey of faith.

WE LIVE OUR FAITH

At Home Each night this week, make a list of ways you have shown in your everyday life that you are a member of the Church. Also make a list of actions that show you are in need of conversion.

In the Parish As a class, participate in celebrating the Baptism of an infant. Prepare for the celebration by asking a parish minister to explain the rite to you.

Born of Water and Spirit

During the Sacrament of Baptism, the priest or deacon blesses the water that will be used in the ceremony. Mighty signs and wonders of God are recalled in the prayer.

With your classmates, pray this prayer based on the Blessing of Water. After each line, respond together, "Blessed are you, O Lord our God!"

PRAYER

God our Father, you give us grace through sacramental signs, which tell us of the wonders of your unseen power.

At the dawn of creation, your Spirit breathed on the waters . . .

You made the waters of the great flood a sign of the end of sin . . .

Through the waters of the Red Sea, you led Israel out of slavery . . .

In the waters of the Jordan, your Son was baptized by John and anointed by the Spirit . . .

Water and blood flowed from Jesus' side as he hung on the cross . . .

In the sacrament of Baptism, may all those you have created in your likeness be cleansed from sin and rise to a new birth by water and the Holy Spirit.

CHAPTER 15

Answering God's Call

PRAYER

We hear you calling us, Lord. Strengthen us to answer your call in lives of loving service.

Listen. God is calling you. That call came first in Baptism. It will continue to come to you in many ways throughout your life. It is a call to serve God and others, and every choice you make every day is an answer.

When you use your talent for sports or your gift for music, you are answering God's call. When you see a need in the world and do something to meet it, you are answering God's call. When you wonder what you'll be when you grow up, you are imagining your answer. As an adult you may choose to answer God's call as a single person, a priest, a married person, or a member of a religious community.

Another word for call is **vocation**. Every one of us has a vocation—a call from God to serve.

ACTIVITY

Draw a picture of yourself using a gift or talent God gave you. Tell how you could use that gift or talent to serve God and others.

Priests and deacons, mothers and fathers, men and women religious, single people—all are needed to do God's work. Everyone's gifts are important in a world in which the needs are so great. Each of us is called to serve God by sharing signs of love.

SCRIPTURE STORY
The Harvest

Once Jesus was surrounded by a crowd of people—some sick and lonely, some longing to share their gifts. Jesus' friends tried to turn them away. But Jesus said, "How can I leave even one of these people hurting?"

He looked out past the faces of the crowd toward a field of wheat. The grain was heavy on the stalks, ripe and ready to be picked.

"The harvest is great," Jesus said to his friends. "But there are not enough laborers. Ask the master of the harvest to send more laborers to gather in the grain."

Jesus' friends realized that he was not talking only about the field in the distance. His thoughts were also with the people in front of him, eager to share their gifts, waiting for a sign of God's love.

—based on Matthew 9:35–38

● **What was Jesus describing when he used the image of the field? What image would you use today to describe the same thing?**

How does each of these people live his or her call to serve God and others?

Vocations of Service

People live their answer to God's call in different ways, or states, of life. In the Church there are two states of life—**lay** and **ordained**.

Many people are called to the vocation of marriage and family life, which is celebrated in the Sacrament of Matrimony. Others answer God's call as single people. Some men are called to a vocation of ordained ministry, celebrated in the Sacrament of Holy Orders. The three kinds of ordained ministry are deacon, priest, and bishop. An ordained man is marked forever to serve as Christ's representative.

Some people respond to a call to religious life. There are many communities and orders of religious men (priests, brothers, friars, or monks) and religious women (sisters or nuns). Religious communities may be primarily active, serving needs in the wider community, or **contemplative**, dedicated to lives of prayer and work apart from the world. Some religious men are also called to ordained ministry.

In Baptism we all receive a share in the priestly ministry of Christ. This ministry is different from the ministry of the ordained. We are all called to live out this ministry according to our vocations. People called to married life or ordained ministry live their call with the grace of Sacraments of Service. Single people, including members of religious communities, serve God, too, through the grace of Baptism.

ACTIVITY

With a partner, make a list of ways married people serve God, each other, their children, and the community.

Promises

At Baptism all of us promise to follow Jesus and to serve God and others. We renew these promises each year at Easter as a reminder that we share in the new life of the risen Christ.

The Sacraments of Vocation involve making promises, too. These sacred promises are called **vows**. Ordained people promise to serve the Church as faithful ministers. Deacons and priests promise to follow the authority of the bishop, and bishops promise to exercise their authority in accordance with other bishops and the pope. Most ordained men also promise **celibacy**—to remain unmarried for the sake of the kingdom.

Married people vow to remain faithful and loving to one another throughout their lives. They promise to share sexual love only with one another and to love, care for, and educate the children they may have.

Members of religious communities do not enter into sacramental marriage and most are not ordained. But they, too, make special vows. The most common religious vows are those of *poverty* (to live simply without clinging to material possessions), *chastity* (to live out the gift of sexuality according to one's vocation, in this case as a single religious), and *obedience* (to put God's will first). These three vows are called the **evangelical counsels** because they describe a way of life modeled on the gospel message.

Our Moral Guide

Fidelity, or faithfulness, is a virtue all vocations require. We practice fidelity by keeping our promises, being reliable, and staying true to our best selves.

Catechism, #2101

Why is fidelity important to all vocations?

Sister Paula transformed a chicken coop into this headquarters for her environmental ministry. Why is it important to find creative ways to answer God's call?

Many Ways to Answer

Every vocation has its own story. God calls each person in a unique way, and each person brings his or her own gifts to a life of service. The story of Sister Paula, who lives in a chicken coop, is a good example.

Paula Gonzalez became a Sister of Charity so she could use her gifts to serve others. Sister Paula answers God's call by teaching and by example. She travels to other countries to show people how to build inexpensive homes and farms powered by solar energy. Sister Paula's ministry is helping people become better stewards of creation by using resources well. She calls this "living lightly on the land."

Sister Paula's home and office is an old chicken coop on a farm owned by her religious community. With recycled materials Sister Paula made it warm, comfortable, and welcoming. She is faithful to her call from God, even in a chicken coop.

Landmark   In the Middle Ages members of religious communities lived in monasteries like this one. They gathered for prayer, work, and simple meals. Today men and women religious live in a variety of settings.

In Service to the Community

Both of the Sacraments of Service celebrate the call to minister to others. In these sacraments we celebrate individual people's willingness to dedicate their lives to serving the community with love.

Sacraments of Service

This chart shows key information about Matrimony and Holy Orders.

	Matrimony	Holy Orders
Recipient	Baptized man and woman called to serve as married couple and as parents	Baptized man called to serve as deacon, priest, or bishop
Principal Minister	The couple	Bishop
Witnesses	Priest or deacon, the community	The community
Sacramental Sign	Exchange of promises	Laying on of hands
Basis in Scripture	Mark 10:6–9	Matthew 28:18–20
From the Rite	"Lord, may they pray to you in the community of the Church, and be your witnesses in the world."	"That our brothers may draw closer to Christ and be his witnesses in the world, let us pray to the Lord."

RECALL

What are the three kinds of ordained ministry? Who is the principal minister of the Sacrament of Matrimony? What promises do married people make?

THINK AND SHARE

Which vocations interest you right now? Why?

CONTINUE THE JOURNEY

Write an ad calling people to a life of service. List the qualities needed and the rewards of the job. Then share your ad with a partner.

Wanted: People to Serve

WE LIVE OUR FAITH

At Home Look at the needs of people in your family and neighborhood. Choose one need you can do something about and take action this week.

In the Parish Explore opportunities your parish offers people your age for answering the call to serve God and others. Choose the opportunity that most appeals to you and become involved.

Our Daily Prayer

The **Liturgy of the Hours,** or Divine Office, is a cycle of psalms, readings, and petitions. It is the Church's daily prayer. Priests, religious, and some lay people pray the Liturgy of the Hours. It is an ancient custom to pray the psalms *antiphonally*, with two groups alternating reading or singing the verses.

PRAYER

Form two groups and pray Psalm 100 antiphonally.

**1: Shout joyfully to the LORD, all you lands;
        worship the LORD with cries of gladness;
        come before him with joyful song.**

**2: Know that the LORD is God,
        our maker to whom we belong,
        whose people we are, God's
            well-tended flock.**

**1: Enter the temple gates with praise,
        its courts with thanksgiving.**

**2: Give thanks to God, bless his name;
        good indeed is the LORD.**

Review

Multiple Choice

Write the letter of the choice that best completes the sentence.

_c___ 1. The Holy Spirit guides the pope and the bishops to teach in matters of faith as the Church's **(a)** catechumenate **(b)** initiation **(c)** magisterium **(d)** sponsor.

_a___ 2. Initiation takes time because it is a **(a)** process **(b)** step backward **(c)** liturgy **(d)** vocation.

_a___ 3. Each one of us has a call from God to **(a)** serve **(b)** lead **(c)** marry **(d)** join a religious community.

_c___ 4. We become members of the Church through the Sacraments of Initiation, which are: **(a)** Baptism, Confirmation, and Holy Orders **(b)** Baptism, Reconciliation, and Eucharist **(c)** Baptism and Confirmation **(d)** Baptism, Confirmation, and Eucharist.

_c___ 5. The Church is described as catholic because **(a)** the apostles spread the good news of salvation in Christ **(b)** Christ gave himself up to sanctify it **(c)** it is universal **(d)** it is not Christian.

Matching

Match the meanings in Column A with the correct terms in Column B.

Column A

_c___ 1. Religious community dedicated to prayer and work apart from the world.

_a___ 2. One of the two states of life.

_d___ 3. One, holy, catholic, apostolic.

_e___ 4. Holy oil.

_b___ 5. People chosen to move toward initiation into the Church.

Column B

a. ordained

b. elect

c. contemplative

d. marks of the Church

e. chrism

Share Your Faith

Someone asks you what it means to have a vocation. What do you say?

Show How Far You've Come

Use this graphic organizer to show what you have learned. For each chapter, write the three most important things you remember.

The Church Is a Sacrament

Chapter 13 A Sign to the World	Chapter 14 Steps on Our Journey	Chapter 15 Answering God's Call

What Else Would You Like to Know?

List any questions you still have about the Church as a sacrament.

_____

_____

_____

Continue the Journey

Choose one or more of the following activities to do on your own, with your class, or with your family.

- Look through your Faith Journal pages for Unit Four. Choose your favorite activity and share it with a friend or family member.

- Read a book about someone who served both the Church and the community in his or her vocation.

- Think about where you are on your faith journey. Discuss the next steps you should take with an older family member, your teacher, or a parish staff member.

Following a Star

PRAYER

God the Father, the glorious Light of your Son, Jesus, shines forth to all people. May we shine forth in love and service to others.

What do you see when you look up at the starry sky at night? Travelers in ancient times saw a map in the night sky. The stars showed them the way to their destinations.

One star story is associated with Jesus' birth. According to the Gospel of Matthew, three **magi**, or wise men, from the East saw a new light rise in the sky. The magi had studied the stars and knew how to find their way by them. They also believed that the stars told of human events. When they spotted the bright new star, the magi knew it was an important sign. It was a sign to them that a king had been born, a king for whom people had long been waiting. The star led the magi to the town of Bethlehem. They followed it to the place where the newborn Jesus lay by his mother, Mary. The magi worshiped Jesus as a king and gave him royal gifts of gold, frankincense, and myrrh (*Matthew 2:1–2, 9–11*).

The Magi

The Savior Is Born

Christmas does not end on December 25. The Season of Christmas begins with the Mass of Christmas Eve and concludes with the Feast of Jesus' Baptism. During this season we celebrate the Feast of the **Epiphany**, which recalls the story of the magi's visit.

The word *epiphany* comes from the Greek word for "manifestation," or "showing forth." In his epiphany Jesus was shown as Savior to the whole world.

Two other manifestations of Jesus have traditionally been celebrated at the Epiphany and still are by Eastern Christians. These additional epiphanies are the baptism of Jesus by John the Baptist and Jesus' first sign at Cana, when he changed water into wine. As Catholics we believe that each of these manifestations is part of God's plan of salvation. Each reveals Jesus as the Savior God promised.

The Feast of the Epiphany celebrates the revelation of Jesus, the Light of the World, to all people. First seen by the magi, the Light shines for us all and shows us the way.

How does Jesus, the Light of the World, manifest himself to us today?

The Baptism of Jesus

The Marriage at Cana

Recall

What three manifestations show that Jesus was the Savior for whom people had been waiting?

Think and Share

Why do you think the Church celebrates Christmas as a season rather than as just one day?

Continue the Journey

The magi brought Jesus gifts that kings would offer to other kings. Draw a picture of a gift you would offer the newborn Jesus.

Blanket

He would be cold

We Live Our Faith

At Home Make the Christmas Season last. Plan one simple activity you can do with family members each day from December 24 to the Feast of the Epiphany to keep the Christmas spirit going.

In the Parish Figures representing the magi are traditionally included in the Christmas *crèche*, or nativity scene. As a class, find out the history of your parish's crèche.

The Twelve Days of Christmas

The days from December 26 to January 6 have traditionally been known as "the twelve days of Christmas." Centuries ago European people celebrated Christmas with religious ceremonies on December 25 and saved their gift-giving for the eve of the Epiphany. They called this evening feast *Twelfth Night*.

You may know a Christmas *carol*, or song, about the twelve days of Christmas. The first Christmas carols were tunes to accompany Twelfth Night dancing. Later, people composed Christmas carols with religious themes to be sung in churches and homes during the season.

Singing religious Christmas carols can be a form of prayer. In words and music we retell the story of salvation.

PRAYER

Sing your favorite religious Christmas carols together. Include "We Three Kings," which tells the story of the magi's visit.

CHAPTER 17

Called to God's Kingdom

PRAYER

Jesus, you invite us into the kingdom of God and bless us with every good thing. Help us find happiness in following you.

"I just don't understand," Jason said, his voice choked with hurt. "When I go to make friends or join in a group, the other kids pretend I'm not there or just walk away. What's wrong with me?"

Jason's mother listened patiently. She could feel how much he was hurting. Without saying a word she motioned for Jason to follow her down the hallway to a mirror. She stood him in front of the mirror.

"Is there something wrong with what you see?" she asked as Jason looked at his reflection.

"Why, no, it's me. I see myself."

"And that's a good thing. You see, it's their loss," his mother said. Jason's face broke into a smile, and a smile beamed back at him from the mirror.

ACTIVITY

With a partner, make a list of specific ways to include others in groups and activities at school.

The words Jesus spoke went straight to the root of the people's troubles. The poor, hungry, and powerless suffered terribly next to those who had money, food, and power. Now they heard from Jesus' lips that they counted in the eyes of God. They understood that there was a place for them in God's kingdom.

—based on Matthew 5:1–10

We call the blessings Jesus gave on the mountainside the **Beatitudes**. This name comes from a word that means both "blessed" and "happy." The kinds of people Jesus blesses in the Beatitudes—the poor, the meek, those who mourn—are not necessarily those that the world would call happy or blessed. But they are people whose actions and attitudes reflect God's love. The people Jesus blesses are living signs of God's kingdom.

The Beatitudes send a message to us that true happiness cannot be found in things such as money or popularity. True happiness can be found only by seeking **righteousness**, the attitude of being in the right relationship in God's kingdom. The Beatitudes help us develop the right attitude to make Christian choices in everyday life.

Scripture Signpost

"At the sight of the crowds, his heart was moved with pity for them because they were troubled and abandoned, like sheep without a shepherd."
Matthew 9:36

In what ways was Jesus a shepherd to the crowds?

The people trusted what Jesus said because he gave them hope in spite of their hunger, poverty, and powerlessness.

Making peace is a special challenge in the times in which we live. Jesus blessed the peacemakers and was himself the Prince of Peace. We need to remind ourselves of Jesus' call to peace in all our dealings with each other.

Catechism, #2305

How can we be peacemakers at home and in school?

We do not have to be poor, hungry, or powerless to live the Beatitudes. It is our attitude about ourselves in relation to God that is important. As Christians we believe that everything is a gift. We see ourselves and others as made in God's image. This attitude is at the heart of our Christian **morality**, the way we put into practice what we believe. The everyday choices and decisions we make reflect our morality.

We are children of God, and we have the love of God as well as many other blessings. Our challenge in living the Beatitudes is to remember who we are and what we have. We receive all kinds of messages from the world around us about who we should be and what we need to have. We face pressures and problems. The Beatitudes help remind us of our attitude, our way of thinking, and our way of living in relationship in the kingdom of God. They remind us that we are blessed and give us hope.

ACTIVITY

With a partner, choose a Beatitude and make a list of the attitudes in society that work *against* that Beatitude. Then come up with one way you can overcome those negative attitudes.

THEY WILL KNOW WE ARE CHRISTIANS BY OUR LOVE

LOVE ONE ANOTHER

Making Moral Decisions

Every day we make choices about how to behave. As people of faith we can turn to teachings of Jesus such as the Beatitudes for help in making choices between right and wrong.

Here are some steps to follow:

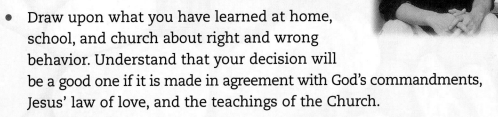

- Remember who you are. You are a child of God. You are not alone in making this decision. The moral values you have been taught will guide you in making a good choice.

- Draw upon what you have learned at home, school, and church about right and wrong behavior. Understand that your decision will be a good one if it is made in agreement with God's commandments, Jesus' law of love, and the teachings of the Church.

- Listen to what your conscience is telling you. Pray to the Holy Spirit for help in deciding what to do.

- Focus on your *motive*—why you want to do one thing or the other. Put the emphasis on the good you are able to do in the present situation.

- Pay attention to your feelings as well as your thoughts. Both play an important part in shaping decisions.

- Afterwards, reflect on and evaluate the consequences of your decision. How did what you decided affect those with whom you live, work, and go to school? How did your decision help others experience the reign of God?

Where Will This Lead Me?

Reviewing these steps now will help you make good moral decisions in the future.

RECALL

What do we call the blessings Jesus gave on the mountainside? What is morality?

THINK AND SHARE

What difference do you think it would make in the world if everyone followed the Beatitudes?

CONTINUE THE JOURNEY

Design an advertisement for the real happiness we find in God's kingdom.

WE LIVE OUR FAITH

At Home With a family member, review the steps for making moral decisions. Talk over any choices you are facing right now.

In the Parish As a class, put together an illustrated booklet showing ways your parish community lives the Beatitudes.

Blessed Are We

It is not easy to live the Beatitudes, but it is worth the effort. And we can always ask for God's help in prayer.

PRAYER

Take turns reading the numbered lines. Pray the response to each line together.

1. Lord, keep us from becoming too attached to material things . . .
   Blessed are we who are poor in spirit!

2. Teach us to share others' sorrow and to be generous with our joy . . .
   Blessed are we who mourn!

3. Keep us from bullying and bragging . . .
   Blessed are we who are meek!

4. Don't let us settle for anything less than your kingdom of justice . . .
   Blessed are we who hunger and thirst for righteousness!

5. Help us let go of the grudges we hold . . .
   Blessed are we who are merciful!

6. Open our eyes to what is good and true in ourselves and in others . . .
   Blessed are we who are clean of heart!

7. Let violence and hatred have no place in our lives . . .
   Blessed are we who are peacemakers!

8. Keep us always faithful to your call, even when it is difficult . . .
   Blessed are we, Lord, for your kingdom belongs to us!

CHAPTER 18

Our Call to Do Good

PRAYER

Gracious God, lead us to become fully ourselves. Teach us to do good as we make our way toward everlasting life with you.

There was once a young man named Phil. Phil loved his job and all his possessions. But something was missing. Then Phil met Sophie. Phil and Sophie spent hours talking. They shared their thoughts and feelings about everything. Phil discovered Sophie had a great gift. She was very wise. The more time Phil spent with Sophie, the more he learned about himself. Sophie brought out the best in Phil. He felt that he could really be himself with her. He had never been happier, and his life had never been richer. Over time Phil and Sophie grew to love each other. They joined their lives in marriage.

If you join the names *Phil* and *Sophie*, you get *philosophy*. Philosophy means "love of wisdom."

134 : We Are Invited

Becoming Who We Really Are

The story of Phil and Sophie shows how love and wisdom can bring out the best in a person. When we become the best we can be, we become who God calls us to be. We can give the best of ourselves to life and others.

We want to be our best selves because that is part of God's plan for us. God calls us to do good, and **virtue** helps us respond to God's call. Virtue is a constant, firm choice to do good. It allows us to give the best of ourselves.

Wisdom is one virtue that can help us do good. By itself, however, wisdom is not enough. Other virtues help guide us in our daily lives.

ACTIVITY

List two ways you can do good in your own home or neighborhood. Trade lists with a partner and try out each other's ideas.

Pictures of Virtue

Four virtues play an especially important role in our lives. They are prudence, justice, fortitude, and temperance. Because of their importance, they are called the **cardinal virtues**. All other human virtues revolve around them.

In every age of our Church's community, there have been people whose lives were examples of virtue. The stories of their lives make the cardinal virtues come alive for us.

A Man of Good Judgment

Thomas More had it all—a wonderful family, a successful career, and the friendship of the king of England. He knew what the good life was. He also knew what it was not. Thomas's ability to see the difference was a sign of his **prudence**, or good judgment in action. Thomas was a lawyer who applied the law wisely so that it served both God and his country. When the king demanded that Thomas show loyalty to him above the Church, however, he could not do what the king asked. Saint Thomas More put God's will above everything and gave his life for his faith.

A Caring and Just Man

Saint Martín de Porres was born in Peru, the son of a Spanish noble and a free black woman. Because of his mixed background, he suffered great injustice. Yet in spite of his experience, he chose to act justly toward others. **Justice** means making sure all people have what is due to them as children of God. Martín learned about medicine and helped poor people who were sick. He had a special ministry to the African people brought to Peru in slavery. As a religious brother, he continued to serve and care for people from all walks of life.

ACTIVITY

Write a short profile of a person who is a model to you of one of the cardinal virtues.

A Woman of Courage

Elizabeth Seton's family thought she had lost her mind after the death of her husband. A widow with five children and no money, she wanted to become a Catholic. In the eyes of many colonial Americans, becoming a Catholic was a disgraceful step. But Elizabeth found comfort in the Catholic Church, and in turn she gave the Church her great energy and strength. Elizabeth became a teacher. She founded some of the first American Catholic schools and brought other women together in a religious community to serve the poor. Through all her struggles Elizabeth never lost heart. Her **fortitude**, or ability to do what is good with courage, carried her through.

A Woman of Balance

Jane Frances de Chantal knew that life had its ups and downs. She was a rich woman, but she knew that many people in her city were poor and hungry. When Jane's beloved husband died, she decided to use her time and her money serving the poor. With help from her friend Francis de Sales, a priest and spiritual writer, Jane formed a group of women like herself to serve the poor. They called themselves *Visitines*, after Mary's visit to her cousin Elizabeth (*Luke 1:39–56*).

When some people in her community wanted to fast too strictly or work all night, Saint Jane Frances urged them to practice **temperance**, the virtue of keeping all things in good balance. "The Lord is more pleased when we accept the relief our body and spirit need," she said, "than when we waste time worrying that we are not doing enough."

Our Moral Guide

Conscience is our connection with God at the center of our being. Like a voice from God, our conscience guides us, telling us when and how to do good.

Catechism, #1776

How can we form our conscience in order to make good decisions?

We can turn to many people for help in doing what is good and right. Whom would you ask for guidance in practicing virtues?

Making Virtue a Habit

A life of virtue does not come easily. We must learn and live virtues until they become *habits*. That is, we must practice them until they are at home within us, until they are a natural part of us.

Many situations in our lifetimes offer us the opportunity to practice the cardinal virtues. Consider the challenges these young people face. Imagine what you would do in their place.

Where Is Justice?

Tina and Justin were arguing. "It's not right," Justin said. "I don't see why that new kid gets to go on the class picnic with us. We worked all year to raise the money for this trip, and he just showed up last week! Besides, he doesn't know anybody and he can't even speak English!"

"His name is Phan," Tina said. "And he does too speak English. But even if he didn't, who cares? He's part of our class now, so he should come with us."

- Which side of the argument reflects the virtue of justice? Why?

A Prudent Choice?

Josh and Kevin were in the mall. Kevin wanted a new CD, but he didn't have the money to buy it. "So just take it," Josh said. "No one will see you." "But that's stealing," Kevin said. "Not really," Josh said. "They overcharge for this stuff anyway, so they'll never miss it."

- How could the virtue of prudence help Kevin decide what to do?

It Takes Courage

"Try it," said Charlie, holding out the tube of glue to Sam. "Just sniff it. It's no big deal." The other boys looked to see how Sam would react. The rest of them had all taken the older boy's dare to sniff the glue. Charlie laughed at Sam. "What are you, a chicken?"

● **What would you do or say if you were Sam?**

Out of Balance

Lisa's two best friends were driving her crazy. Amy ate every bit of junk food she could get her hands on. She was always stuffing herself with fries, chips, and candy bars. Jenny was just the opposite. Even though she was thin, Jenny was always dieting and exercising. "Oh, that's just disgusting," she would say when Lisa ordered a hamburger.

● **Which virtue do Lisa's friends need help practicing? How should she help them?**

These scenes probably remind you of situations you have experienced. Just remember that virtues such as prudence, justice, fortitude, and temperance help us act for good. When we do, we are becoming who we really are—we are becoming the kind of people God wants us to be.

RECALL

What is virtue? What are the four cardinal virtues?

THINK AND SHARE

How are stories of saints who lived particular virtues useful to us?

CONTINUE THE JOURNEY

Make a collage of the four cardinal virtues. Divide a sheet of paper into four sections, one for each virtue. Collect magazine pictures of people trying to live each virtue to include in each section.

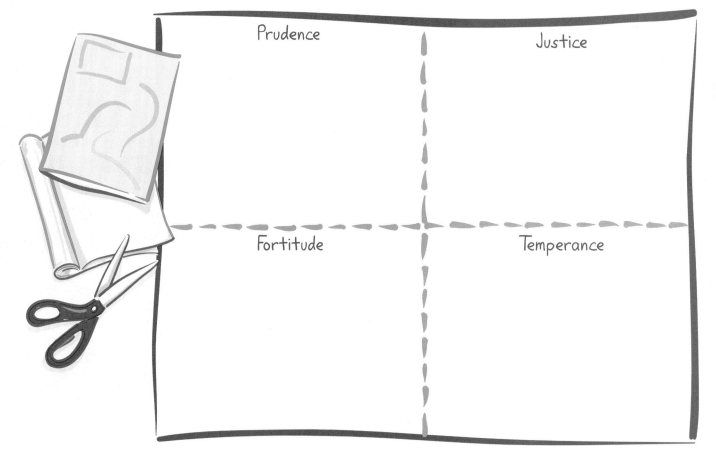

Prudence

Justice

Fortitude

Temperance

WE LIVE OUR FAITH

At Home Select one of the four cardinal virtues and look for ways to practice it at home. Keep a journal of your experiences for a week or two.

In the Parish Participate in a school or parish retreat, day of prayer, or Reconciliation service to improve your practice of the habits of virtue.

Where Can We Turn?

Sometimes, leading a good moral life can seem impossible. Everywhere we turn, we see other ways to be and act that are very different from the Christian way. We need to remember that God is with us. God will give us the gift of wisdom, from which all other virtues flow.

**"What is more rich than Wisdom,
who produces all things?
For she teaches temperance and prudence,
justice and courage."**

—based on Wisdom 8:5, 7

Prayer

Pray together this prayer based on King Solomon's request for wisdom.

**Lord of mercy, you who made all things with
your word,
Give us Wisdom
for she knows and understands all things,
and will guide us in our choices, and keep
us safe.
Then our actions will be acceptable to you.
Our way will be clear, and our path will
be straight,
and we will be saved.**

—based on Wisdom 9:1, 4, 11, 18

CHAPTER 19
Forgiveness and Healing

PRAYER

Jesus, you love to forgive and heal people who have faith in you. Draw us closer to your forgiving touch in the Sacraments of Healing.

Take a look. Are any of these scenes familiar? Can you identify with what any of the people here are experiencing? Now take a closer look. Suppose you have been asked to label these pictures. You may use the label *Forgiveness* or the label *Healing.* How would you label each?

How did you label the photos? Some of the pictures probably made you think about how much forgiveness and healing are alike. Both forgiveness and healing restore us. They work to make us whole again. Forgiveness makes us whole again when we have been damaged by sin. Healing makes us whole again when we have suffered from sickness.

Because we are human, we cannot escape sin or sickness. We can, however, find forgiveness and healing in the Church. In our Church community the care of the whole person, soul and body, is first celebrated in the forgiving and healing waters of Baptism. Two other sacraments of the Church—Reconciliation and the Anointing of the Sick—continue Jesus' work of forgiveness and healing. Christ reaches out to us through these healing signs, helping us become whole again.

ACTIVITY

Draw a scene of healing or forgiveness that could be added to these pictures.

SCRIPTURE STORY
A Generous Father

Like any good teacher, Jesus told stories. To show that God's forgiveness has no limits, he told this story.

A man had two sons. The younger one wanted to be on his own. He asked his father for his inheritance, and his father gave it to him willingly.

It did not take the son long to spend all the money his father had given him. Penniless, he wound up working on a farm feeding pigs. The young man was so hungry he could have eaten the slop fed to the pigs. Then one day he came to his senses. He thought, "I'll return to my father's house and work there as a servant."

As the son approached his father's house, the father saw him, ran to him, and hugged and kissed him. "Father, I have sinned against heaven and against you," the son stammered. "I'm not worthy to be called your son." The father called his servants. He told them to bring fine clothes for his son and to prepare a great feast to celebrate his homecoming. "My son who was dead has come back to life," the father explained. "He was lost, and now he has been found." Then the celebration began.

—based on Luke 15:11–24

● **What do you think the father meant when he described his son as dead and lost?**

ACTIVITY

Make up a version of the story of the generous father that is set in the present day. Tell it to your classmates.

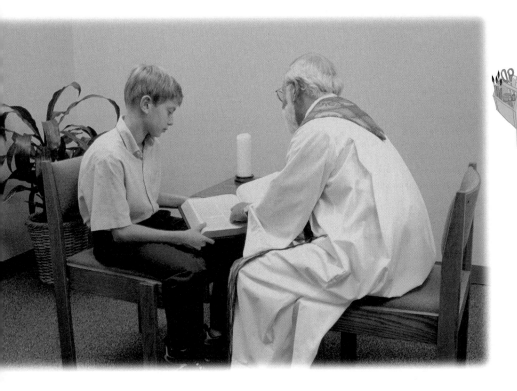

ACTIVITY

Write a prayer of contrition in your own words. Express your love for God and tell God and the community that you are sorry for what you have done.

Always Welcome

Like the father in the story Jesus told, God always wants us to come home and is willing to wait for our return. If you think the father in the story may have been too forgiving, then imagine this: God, our heavenly Father, is even more forgiving toward us.

We are never far from God's mercy. Once we are truly sorry for our sins, we can express our sorrow in a visible and sacramental way. We can come home to God. Our homecoming can take place in the Eucharist, through *perfect contrition,* and in the Sacrament of Reconciliation.

When members of the Church commit serious sin, they are expected to celebrate the Sacrament of Reconciliation. Reconciliation heals our wounded relationships with God, others, and the Church. It brings us peace and the strength to do good. Any sins confessed in this sacrament can never be told to anyone by the priest.

The power of God's mercy and forgiveness transforms us. We were dead, but now we are alive again. We were lost, but now we have been found.

Our Moral Guide

Contrition is the sorrow that fills our hearts when we have sinned. It is a first step in the healing process. Contrition moves us to seek God's forgiveness and contributes to our resolve not to sin again.

Catechism, #1451

Why is contrition an important part of the healing process?

A Life-Giving Touch

Like the Sacrament of Reconciliation, the Sacrament of the Anointing of the Sick is a healing sign. The Anointing of the Sick brings strength to those who have been weakened by sickness, suffering, or old age. As this story shows, it offers a life-giving touch that is a blessing.

After she had a stroke, Great-Aunt Margie moved in with us. The doctors told her she had to slow down and start taking care of herself. She obeyed their orders except when it came to going to Mass each day. Nothing could keep her from walking the few blocks to St. Patrick's.

The Anointing of the Sick brings members of the Church together.

One night, Aunt Margie had a special request. "Hannah, would you come with me to Mass in the morning?" she asked. "Father Ted is going to anoint some of us. Your mom will come along with us."

I was concerned. Didn't anointing mean you were dying or something? Smiling, Aunt Margie squeezed my hand and reassured me.

"Nothing to worry about, Hannah," she said. "These blessings are what keep me going."

The next morning Mom and I stood with Great-Aunt Margie as she and some other parishioners received the Anointing of the Sick. It made me feel good to be a part of something that kept Aunt Margie feeling strong and happy.

Sacraments of Healing

Our new life in Christ can be renewed or found again through the Sacraments of Healing.

	Reconciliation	The Anointing of the Sick
Purpose	To restore a person to God and the Church after he or she has been separated from them by sin	To offer the healing touch of Christ to an ill or suffering person
Preparation	The individual who has sinned is moved to turn to God. The person examines his or her conscience.	The ill or suffering individual turns to God and the Church to receive Christ's touch. The Sacrament of Reconciliation may be celebrated as part of the preparation.
Celebration	• The individual is greeted and blessed by the priest. • A brief passage from Scripture is read. • The person confesses his or her sins to the priest. The priest listens and offers counsel. • The priest gives the individual an appropriate penance. The person resolves not to sin again and asks for God's help. • The priest forgives and absolves the individual in the name of Christ and his Church.	• The sacrament is often celebrated when the community is gathered for the Eucharist. Other settings are also possible. • A brief passage from Scripture is read. • The priest lays hands on the person, prays over him or her, and anoints the person with oil blessed by the bishop. • Family members and parishioners join in the prayers and responses.

RECALL

How are forgiveness and healing alike? What are the Sacraments of Healing?

THINK AND SHARE

How do you think members of the Church can help those who have sinned and sought forgiveness?

CONTINUE THE JOURNEY

Take time to make an examination of conscience. Then draw a picture of an act of kindness you could perform to make up for some wrong you have done.

WE LIVE OUR FAITH

At Home Make a card for a family member who is always there for you. In the card, tell the person how much his or her love and support mean to you.

In the Parish As a class, attend a parish celebration of the Anointing of the Sick. In your class prayers, remember those who are anointed.

OJCZE, ZGRZESZYŁEM
ŁUK. 15-21

Forgive Our Sins

The Sacrament of Reconciliation may be celebrated individually or communally. In either case, the confession and absolution are private. A litany of contrition is part of the communal celebration of Reconciliation.

Pray this litany together.

PRAYER

God our Father, sometimes we have not behaved
as your children . . .
But you love us and come to us.

We have given trouble to our parents and teachers . . .

We have quarreled and called each other names . . .

We have been lazy at home and in school, and we have
not been helpful to our families and our friends . . .

We have thought too much of ourselves and have
told lies . . .

We have not done good to others when we had
the chance . . .

Now with Jesus, our Brother, we come before our
Father in heaven and ask him to forgive our sins.

Our Father . . .

—from the Rite of Penance

Review

Matching
Match the meanings in Column A with the correct terms in Column B.

Column A

_b_ 1. Prudence, justice, fortitude, temperance.

_e_ 2. Quality of our character that guides us to do good.

_d_ 3. Blessings Jesus gave on the mountain.

_a_ 4. Natural, regular part of our behavior.

_c_ 5. Sorrow that fills our heart when we have sinned.

Column B

a. habit

b. cardinal virtues

c. contrition

d. Beatitudes

e. virtue

Complete the Sentence
Select the term that best completes each sentence.

1. Another word used to describe fortitude is (courage, ~~fairness~~).

2. (Attitude, ~~Conscience~~) is the way we think about ourselves and our experiences.

3. The Beatitudes show us paths to the (~~cardinal virtues,~~ kingdom of heaven).

4. When we practice temperance, we find (~~enemies,~~ balance) in our lives.

5. We seek (~~penance,~~ forgiveness) from God and the community in the Sacrament of Reconciliation.

Share Your Faith
You hear someone say that Catholics do not really have to make moral decisions; they just do whatever the Church tells them to do. How would you help this person better understand how we come to decisions about moral issues?

Show How Far You've Come
Use this chart to show what you have learned. For each chapter, write the three most important things you remember.

The Life of Grace

Chapter 17 Called to God's Kingdom	Chapter 18 Our Call to Do Good	Chapter 19 Forgiveness and Healing

What Else Would You Like to Know?
List any questions you still have about how we can answer God's call to holiness and wholeness.

_____

_____

_____

Continue the Journey
Choose one or more of the following activities to do on your own, with your class, or with your family.

- Look through your Faith Journal pages for Unit Five. Choose your favorite activity and share it with a friend or family member.

- Find ways to do small things at school or in your neighborhood to bring about justice and peace.

- Read newspapers and magazines to find stories about people whose lives are models of the cardinal virtues. Try to identify an example of each virtue. Clip the articles and write a short paragraph about each person that explains how he or she practices one of the virtues.

THE SEASON OF

PRAYER

Jesus, be with us as we journey this Lent. Turn our hearts toward God and one another as we seek to renew the promises made at Baptism.

Have you ever gone on a journey? A real journey is more than just getting from one place to another. It's a kind of adventure in which the things that happen to us along the road can change our lives.

Lent, the 40-day season of preparation for Easter, is a journey. During Lent the Church calls us to do penance for our sins and to embrace the good news as the way of salvation. This call can be seen in a positive light. We can answer it by moving in a positive direction, with prayer and works of charity.

You might choose to devote more time to studying, for example, instead of talking on the phone or watching television. You might volunteer to help out at home instead of waiting to be asked to do your part. The 40 days of Lent need not be seen just as a time of giving up or doing without.

Through a positive attitude and positive actions, the Season of Lent can be a time of giving and searching within. It is a time of **conversion**, a time of turning to God in Christ.

We meet Jesus on our Lenten journey. One Lenten gospel reading tells the story of Jesus' meeting with a Samaritan woman *(John 4:42)*. What did Jesus ask of the woman? What did he offer her?

CONVERSION

JOURNEYING TOGETHER

The journey of conversion that we travel during Lent should never be seen as a lonely journey. Lent is a time to walk together. We have companions for the journey. The root meaning of the word *companion* is "someone with whom bread is shared." In our Church that bread is the Bread of Life in the Eucharist. We share our bread and our journey with others in the Church.

In the early Church the entire community joined in the preparations for the great feast of Easter. The faithful, who had already been baptized, joined with the *elect*, those who were preparing to be initiated into the Church. All fasted and purified their hearts and souls through prayer and sacrifice.

Today members of the Church still travel a journey of conversion with the elect during Lent. During a time of reflection toward the end of Lent, the elect make final preparations for receiving the Easter sacraments. All in the community of the Church—elect and members together—search their hearts and minds. The purpose of this soul-searching is to find and root out whatever stands in the way of our turning away from sin and to God. With God's grace all prepare for the great feast of Easter.

Catholics Believe . . .

that the Season of Lent invites us to look into our hearts, do penance willingly, and purify ourselves in order to give ourselves totally to God.

Catechism, #1428

ACTIVITY

In a small group, make a list of positive actions you can take during Lent. Share your ideas with your teacher and other classmates.

RECALL

What do we call the 40 days before Easter during which the Church turns to God in prayer and penance? What is conversion?

THINK AND SHARE

Why do you think we take time at Lent to turn to God?

CONTINUE THE JOURNEY

Chart your journey of conversion during Lent. Make a spiritual calendar for the season. Mark where you go, what you do, with whom you spend time, and other experiences during the days of Lent.

		Ash Wednesday		
1st Sunday of Lent				
2nd Sunday of Lent				
3rd Sunday of Lent				
4th Sunday of Lent				
5th Sunday of Lent				
Palm/Passion Sunday		Holy Thursday	Good Friday	Holy Saturday

WE LIVE OUR FAITH

At Home Help a family member without being asked, or suggest doing something you know others in your family would like to do, such as playing a board game or going for a bike ride.

In the Parish Attend a parish celebration of one of the *scrutinies*, the special celebrations for the elect held on three Lenten Sundays.

ON OUR LENTEN JOURNEY

During Lent we join with the elect, those preparing for Baptism at Easter, in a journey of conversion. Our prayer for these newest members of our community can be a prayer for ourselves, too.

Remember all those preparing for the Sacraments of Initiation as you pray together.

PRAYER

**During this Season of Lent, Lord,
may we find joy in daily prayer;
may we joyfully read your word and ponder it in
    our hearts;
may we humbly confess our faults and
    energetically begin to correct them;
may we turn our daily actions into an offering
    pleasing to you;
may we grow in love and seek virtue and
    holiness of life;
and may we be more concerned for others than
    for ourselves.
Protect and bless our families, Lord,
and all who travel this Lenten journey with us.**

—*based on a prayer from the Rite of Election*

CHAPTER 21

Gathered Around the Altar

PRAYER

Lord Jesus, you call us to be a holy people, a worshiping people. In your goodness, Spirit of Christ, bring us together to give praise to your heavenly Father.

Dorothy Day School Journal

May 14, 2056

PRESIDENT TO VISIT OUR SCHOOL

We have begun to prepare for the president's visit. The school building has been thoroughly checked by the Secret Service. At last week's assembly each grade was assigned a special task to make the event memorable. The first and second graders will work together to make welcome signs. Third and fourth graders will help decorate the school auditorium with red, white, and blue streamers and balloons.

The fifth graders chose two girls and two boys to greet the president. An honor guard of students in the sixth and seventh grades will carry the American flag, the state flag, and the *papal* flag in the procession into the auditorium. A chorus of eighth graders will lead everyone in singing our national anthem.

The principal will represent everyone in the school—students, teachers, parents, and staff. In our name the principal will welcome President Gloria Díaz back to her old elementary school.

Together in One Place

None of us may ever have such an honored guest visit our community. Yet we can learn something from the special occasion at Dorothy Day School. Everyone, from the youngest students to the principal, had a role to play in the event. Everyone participated. The day was special because the president of the United States was coming to visit. It was also special because the entire school came together to prepare for the event. Both the presence of the president and the assembly of the entire school made the time and place special.

People gather in different places at different times for various reasons. Every week we gather as a worshiping people in our parish. We prepare to celebrate the presence of Christ among us. We make preparations so that we know who will do what and when. When we *assemble,* or come together, all of us have roles to play. We want to participate willingly, intelligently, and joyfully in the liturgy, especially the Eucharist.

ACTIVITY

Think of a special occasion you experienced with your family or classmates. List people who were present and the parts they played in making the event special.

SCRIPTURE STORY
Building Up God's Church

On his travels the apostle Paul helped start a small Christian community in the Greek city of Corinth. Some time later, as he journeyed farther east, Paul heard that there was trouble among the Christians in Corinth. Arguments had broken out. The small community of faith had begun to split into even smaller groups following different leaders. Some thought they were better than others because they could speak in unknown *tongues*, or languages. Others acted as though the teachings of Christ were for only a few special people, not for all.

Worse still, the arguing had spread to the worshiping assembly. Some members of the assembly were rude to others and tried to leave people out. The Eucharist was no longer celebrated as the sign of unity it was meant to be.

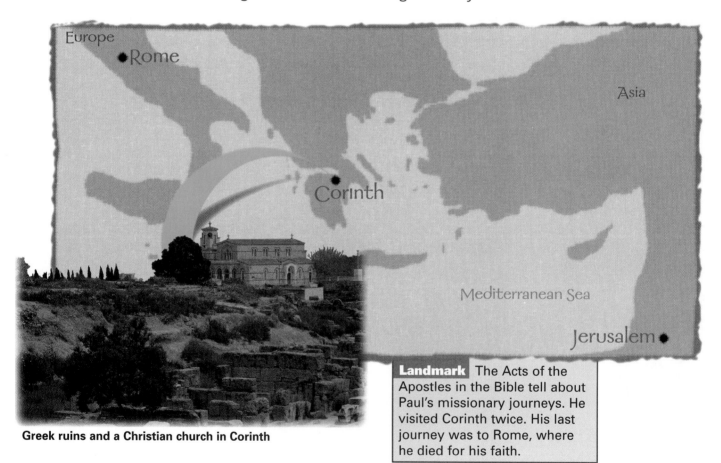

Europe

Rome

Asia

Corinth

Mediterranean Sea

Jerusalem

Greek ruins and a Christian church in Corinth

Landmark The Acts of the Apostles in the Bible tell about Paul's missionary journeys. He visited Corinth twice. His last journey was to Rome, where he died for his faith.

ACTIVITY

What helps you remember that the time and place in which we gather for worship are sacred? Draw a picture or compose a short saying or phrase as a reminder to yourself.

It seemed to Paul that everything he had helped build in Corinth was in danger. He sat down immediately and wrote a letter to the Corinthians. In the letter Paul explained what needed to be done. He gave specific instructions for the assembly regarding worship. "When you assemble," Paul wrote, "one person should prepare the psalm. Another should explain it. Others should help the community understand how God is speaking to you."

Paul knew that the Corinthians had many gifts to share in the assembly. It was the way they used their gifts, though, that made a difference. Everything that was done, Paul told the Corinthians, should be done for building up the community.

—*based on 1 Corinthians 14:20–28*

Paul understood that many of the Christians in Corinth had forgotten why they had gathered together. They had begun to use the time and place of the assembly for their own purposes. They needed to be reminded that the time and place of the assembly were set apart to honor God. The time, the place, and the gathered people were **sacred**.

Scripture Signpost

"For as in one body we have many parts, and all the parts do not have the same function, so we, though many, are one body of Christ and individually parts of one another."
Romans 12:4–5

How are the members of the Body of Christ, or the community of faith, like the parts of the body?

Our Moral Guide

We have an **obligation**, or duty, to honor God. We honor God by taking part in the liturgy and receiving the Eucharist each Sunday and *holy day*.

Catechism, #2181

Which commandment reminds us of our duty to participate in the Eucharist?

All Have a Role

One way we can help build up the Church is by taking an active role in the gathering for the Eucharist, or **Eucharistic assembly**.

All of us take part in the celebration, each in our own way. We do this first of all by the attitude we bring to the celebration. Throughout the Eucharist we in the assembly are more than observers. We take an active part and all of the actions have meaning.

Certain members are called to special service as ordained ministers—bishops, priests, and deacons. Through the power of the Holy Spirit, bishops and priests *preside,* or act as the head of the assembly. In this role they act in the person of Christ, who is the invisible head of the Church. Other members of the assembly also help make the Eucharistic gathering meaningful. Because they contribute in a particular way to the liturgy, they are called **liturgical ministers**.

The choir and other musicians, the **lectors** who proclaim the assigned readings, the altar servers, and the Eucharistic ministers all play their roles in our celebration.

Whatever we do as a gathered people of God is holy. In the Eucharist we *testify* to God's holiness and strengthen one another under the guidance of the Holy Spirit.

If you could take the role of any of the people shown, which would you choose? Explain your choice.

Preparing for Mass

The Mass is the center of our life. To fully appreciate it, we must prepare. This preparation will help you participate more actively and reverently.

Here are steps to follow:

- Think of the Mass as a continuing and real part of your life, not as a separate event that happens at the beginning of each week.

- Invite family members or friends to attend Mass with you to share the experience and a sense of community.

- Arrive early enough to look over the readings. Listen carefully to the homily to understand how the readings illustrate a common theme.

- Remember to use all five of your senses throughout the celebration to be aware of all the parts of the Mass.

- Note the different rhythms of the Mass. Be aware, for example, of how moments of silence between the readings and after Holy Communion are balanced by singing and group response.

- Remember that you have a key role in the celebration. You are a member of the assembly. Even when you are not carrying out a liturgical ministry, your voice, your body, your prayers, and your presence are important to the celebration of the Mass. Use them to contribute to the community's worship.

Where Will This Lead Me?

Following these steps will help you participate more fully in the Mass and find greater meaning in its celebration.

RECALL

What is the Eucharistic assembly? Who is the head of the
assembly? Who are the various liturgical ministers?

THINK AND SHARE

How do you think young people can take part in the Eucharistic
assembly?

CONTINUE THE JOURNEY

Think of the gifts you bring to the Eucharistic assembly. On
the altar, draw or write about your contribution to the Mass.

WE LIVE OUR FAITH

At Home Talk with your family about how you prepare
for special gatherings. Use some of these steps to prepare
for the Mass this week.

In the Parish Part of belonging to the Eucharistic
assembly is getting to know others. This week, arrive early
for Mass, or stay after Mass, and introduce yourself to
parishioners and parish ministers.

A Song of Gathering

In Jesus' time people would gather in Jerusalem to worship God in the Temple. On their way to the Temple, the people would sing psalms praising God.

We usually begin our celebration of the Eucharist with a gathering *hymn,* or sacred song. Sometimes this entrance hymn is a version of one of the psalms of gathering.

Pray these words from Psalm 95 together. This hymn welcomes God into the assembly. In the same way, at Mass we join together to greet and praise God our Father, Christ his Son, and the Holy Spirit.

PRAYER

Come, let us sing joyfully to the LORD;
    cry out to the rock of our salvation.
Let us greet him with a song of praise,
    joyfully sing out our psalms.
Enter, let us bow down in worship;
    let us kneel before the LORD who made us.
For this is our God,
    whose people we are,
    God's well-tended flock.

—Psalm 95:1–2, 6–7

CHAPTER 22

God's Word Lives

PRAYER

O Most Holy Trinity, you reveal your love and care for us in the inspired words of Scripture. Open our hearts and minds to your word.

Think of your favorite family stories. Family stories tell us about our past and about who we are today. They help us feel connected to our *ancestors,* those generations who lived before us.

How would you feel if someone told you your family stories were lies?

The Christians of second-century Rome knew what that felt like. One of their fellow Christians, a man named Marcion, had made a startling claim.

Marcion wanted the Old Testament, which contained many of the **Hebrew Scriptures**, to be cut out of the Christian Bible. Marcion claimed that the Old Testament showed a hateful and jealous god who created an evil universe. According to Marcion, the God of the Old Testament was not the same God revealed by Jesus Christ. The God of Jesus, revealed in the New Testament, was filled with only love and mercy.

Marcion was an intelligent man. He had studied the Scriptures in their original languages. Many people followed his ideas. But his ideas were wrong, not only because they were an insult to the Jewish people, but also because Marcion was denying a central truth of our faith.

Family stories put us in touch with our history. What family story might you want to pass on to your children and grandchildren?

As Christians we believe that God, our Creator, is all-good. God could not create evil. The God of the Old Testament (the God of Abraham and Sarah, Isaac, and Jacob) is also the God of the New Testament (the Father of Jesus, the God of Mary, Joseph, Elizabeth, Peter, and Paul).

The Church did not accept Marcion's *interpretation,* or understanding, of the Bible. Marcion and his followers refused to give up their claims. Sadly, they cut themselves off from the Body of Christ, the Church.

Our Sacred Scripture

To this day the Church protects and defends the living word of God in the Bible. The Old Testament has 46 books

and the New Testament has 27 books. The two parts of the Bible cannot be divided up to suit someone's opinion. For Christians each is part of the whole. Together the two testaments proclaim faith in the God of Israel who is the Father of Jesus Christ.

The unity of the Old Testament and New Testament is unbreakable. Both are part of our Sacred Scripture. Both are included in the liturgy. During the Mass we hear readings from the Old Testament and from the New Testament. Together they tell the full story of God's promises to the people of Israel and God's revelation in Christ Jesus.

How is the Old Testament like the family story of our faith?

Saints Walk with Us

**Saint Jerome
Feast Day:
September 30**

Saint Jerome translated the books of the Bible into Latin, a language the people of his time could understand. He opened the family story of faith to all Christians.

In art Saint Jerome is often shown with books and a lion. The lion came to be his sign because he lived in the wilderness among wild animals.

Landmark The word *Bible* means "a collection of books." The first Bibles used by the Church were collections of parchment scrolls like these. Scrolls of the Hebrew Scriptures had been used in worship for centuries before the time of Christ. Today Jewish people still read the Scriptures from scrolls in worship.

With Us in God's Word

The words of Scripture don't just mean whatever we want them to mean. They have a rich meaning revealed by God. When we read the Old Testament and the New Testament, we are reading the Church's book. We are surrounded by the whole family of faith every time we tell or hear our story. Just as family stories are handed on from generation to generation, so our understanding of Scripture comes to us from Jesus and the apostles. That understanding, handed on to each new generation of Christians, is called **Tradition**. The word *tradition* means "something passed from hand to hand." Scripture and Tradition together make up the one common source of God's revelation.

Today the living word of God is an important part of our celebration of the sacraments. At every Mass and in the rituals of the sacraments, we hear the good news of salvation in selected readings from Scripture. As we listen, we come to recognize that Jesus is present in the word. He is really with us.

Breaking and Sharing

You know that we share in Christ's Body by breaking and sharing the Bread of Life. In much the same way, we break open and share the word of God in the Scriptures. The way the Church uses the Bible helps us do this.

The selections from the Bible we hear at Mass are collected in the **lectionary**, a book of Scripture readings for use in the liturgy. The lectionary is set up so that the readings for each Sunday are repeated every three years. The choice of readings, and the way they are repeated, is meant to help us become familiar with the richness of Scripture.

On Sundays we hear three readings. The Liturgy of the Word usually opens with a reading from the Old Testament that expresses the theme for the day. We respond to this reading with a psalm, also drawn from the Old Testament. The second reading is taken from the New Testament letters, or *epistles*. This reading need not be connected to the theme of the day. The third reading is from one of the Gospels, usually Matthew, Mark, or Luke. The gospel reading again expresses the day's theme.

Although the other words spoken in the Liturgy of the Word are not from Scripture, they, too, make Jesus present among us. The **homily**, given by the bishop, priest, or deacon, explains what the word of God means in our lives. Jesus is also present as we proclaim our faith by reciting the Creed. He hears our prayers as we remember the needs of the community in the general intercessions.

Scripture Signpost

"All scripture is inspired by God and is useful for teaching. . . ."
2 Timothy 3:16

Why do you think Scripture is an important part of the liturgy?

ACTIVITY

Choose a favorite passage from one of the Gospels. Make up a short talk about how you think God is speaking to people your age through these words.

At the Table of the Word

Everything we do at Mass is meant to join us with Jesus and with the community in praising God. The places we gather for Mass have many different designs, based on history and custom and liturgical laws. But no matter what the worship space may look like, the first part of the Mass centers around the Word of God.

These charts show the movement of the Mass from the introductory rites, when we gather, through the Liturgy of the Word.

The Introductory Rites

- **Gathering Song**

The presider and other liturgical ministers enter in procession as we sing a hymn. If no song is sung, we pray an *antiphon,* or verse, from a psalm.

- **Greeting**

The presider greets us in the name of the Father, and of the Son, and of the Holy Spirit.

- **Rite of Blessing and Sprinkling with Holy Water**

Sometimes the presider blesses holy water at the beginning of Mass. He sprinkles water on the assembly to remind us of our Baptism. We pray that God will cleanse us of our sins.

- **Penitential Rite**

On most Sundays we celebrate the penitential rite to show sorrow for sin. We confess publicly that we have failed to show love to God and to one another. We ask for God's mercy.

- **Glory to God**

We sing or pray an ancient prayer of praise to the Holy Trinity.

- **Opening Prayer**

The presider gathers our prayers and brings them before God. Having asked forgiveness and praised God, we trust God to hear us. We are prepared to hear God speaking to us in the Liturgy of the Word.

The Liturgy of the Word

- **First Reading**

During most of the Church year, the first reading is from the Old Testament. In the Easter Season this reading is taken from the New Testament Acts of the Apostles. This book tells the story of the early Church. We respond to the lector's proclamation, "The word of the Lord," by praying, "Thanks be to God."

- **Responsorial Psalm**

Often a cantor, or song leader, sings the verses of the psalm. We respond by singing the repeated antiphon together.

- **Second Reading**

This reading is taken from one of the letters written by Paul and other apostles, or their followers, to groups of early Christians.

- **Alleluia**

A Scripture verse is proclaimed or sung, and we respond by singing "Alleluia," which is Hebrew for "Praise God!" During the penitential season of Lent, this joyful song is usually replaced by a simple prayer of praise to Jesus, our Savior.

- **Gospel**

Sometimes the gospel book is carried in procession to the ambo. It may be accompanied by ministers carrying lighted candles and burning incense as signs of honor. As the presider or deacon introduces the reading, Catholics traditionally trace the sign of the cross on their foreheads, lips, and hearts. This is our way of praying that God's word will become part of everything we think, say, and love. We stand for the reading of the gospel because standing shows respect. After the gospel reading the presider or deacon kisses the gospel book as another sign of respect. He says, "The gospel of the Lord." We answer, "Praise to you, Lord Jesus Christ."

- **Homily**

The presider or deacon "breaks open" God's word by explaining its meaning for us today. We share the word by making it a part of our lives.

- **The Creed**

In response to the gift of God's word, we stand and proclaim our faith. The words we use, called the Nicene Creed, are more than 1500 years old. This creed, along with a simpler form called the Apostles' Creed, was composed in answer to the false teachings of people like Marcion.

- **General Intercessions**

The presider, deacon, or another liturgical minister leads us in a litany of prayers. We ask God to care for our families, our community, our leaders, and all those who are sick or in need. To each intercession we respond "Lord, hear our prayer."

RECALL

What is a lectionary? What do we call the talk given by the presider or deacon to explain the Scripture readings?

THINK AND SHARE

How is Jesus present in the Liturgy of the Word?

CONTINUE THE JOURNEY

Design a reminder to help you pay attention to Scripture in the Liturgy of the Word.

WE LIVE OUR FAITH

 At Home Find out what readings from the Bible will be used next Sunday. Read these Bible passages ahead of time and talk about what they mean with a family member.

In the Parish Pay attention to the general intercessions at Mass. For whom are the members of your faith community praying?

Open Our Eyes

To see how the parts of the Liturgy of the Word work together, you can celebrate your own Scripture service.

The suggestions below are taken from the Mass for the Seventeenth Sunday in Ordinary Time, Cycle A of the Lectionary. The theme of these readings and prayers is the search for God's presence in our world. After you pray the opening prayer and share the readings, talk about what the words mean to you.

PRAYER

God our Father, open our eyes to see your hand at work in the splendor of creation, in the beauty of human life. Touched by your hand, our world is holy.
Help us cherish the gifts that surround us,
share your blessings with our brothers and sisters,
and experience the joy of life in your presence.
We ask this through Christ our Lord. Amen.

First Reading: 1 Kings 3:5, 7–12 (King Solomon asks for the gift of wisdom.)

Responsorial Psalm: Psalm 119 (Antiphon: "Lord, I love your commands.")

Second Reading: Romans 8:28–30 (God makes all things work for our good.)

Alleluia Verse: Matthew 11:25

Gospel Reading: Matthew 13:44–52 (Jesus tells parables of the reign of God.)

CHAPTER 23

We Celebrate the Eucharist

PRAYER

Lord Jesus, our eternal high priest, you lead us in the perfect sacrifice of praise at the feast of the Eucharist. Through the Holy Spirit, make us members of your Body.

During the 1930s Americans suffered through the Great Depression. It was a dark and difficult time for many, including perhaps the families of your great-grandparents. Crops failed and factories shut down. Farmers lost their farms as dry conditions turned their fields into a "dust bowl." Others lost their jobs and could no longer afford their homes. Many people were uprooted and had to live on the streets, in shacks, even in railroad cars. Many had no money for food, if there was food to be had.

People stood in long lines to wait for handouts of bread. These "bread lines" were often many blocks long. Mothers with hungry children waited patiently. Men without work shuffled in the shadows, their heads bowed in shame. They desperately needed something, anything, to eat. On one bread line many people's situation was summed up in these simple but strong words: "Without this bread, we're dead."

ACTIVITY

Name some ways your parish reaches out to the hungry in your community.

The Bread of Life

People's hunger for bread in the 1930s was real. Now, as then, people hunger for another kind of bread. We hunger for the Bread of Life in the Eucharist. This hunger is just as real as physical hunger. As humans we hunger for happiness. Only God can feed this hunger, for God alone is the source of true happiness. God gave us a taste of true happiness in Jesus our Savior.

In the Sacrament of the Eucharist, we share the Bread of Life and the Cup of Salvation. We taste the happiness we will one day experience fully with God in heaven. The bread we eat at meals and the Bread of Life in the Eucharist are similar. Both offer nourishment and life. The Bread of the Eucharist, however, offers lasting spiritual nourishment and the promise of eternal life.

Scripture Signpost

"I am the living bread that came down from heaven; whoever eats this bread will live forever; and the bread that I will give is my flesh for the life of the world."

John 6:51

How do you think the bread that Jesus gives becomes the life of the world?

Catholics Believe . . .

that in the Eucharist we receive Christ, who offered himself for the life of the world.

Catechism, #1355

Scripture Story
While They Were Eating

Jesus knew that the time had come. With him at the table were his closest friends, the apostles. Jesus wanted to be present with them always and in a special way. With simple words and actions, Jesus gave new meaning to the religious meal they were sharing.

Jesus took bread, said the blessing, and broke it. He gave it to his disciples and said, "Take and eat; this is my body." Then he took a cup, gave thanks, and gave it to them. He said, "Drink from it, all of you, for this is my blood of the covenant, which will be shed on behalf of many for the forgiveness of sins."

Jesus shared himself in anticipation of his death and resurrection. He commanded his friends, "Do this in memory of me." Jesus wanted them to continue to come together when they were hungry. He wanted them to gather in memory of him. Every time they gathered at the table and broke bread and drank wine, he would be present and active in their midst.

—based on Matthew 26:26–27; Luke 22:19–20

Jesus told the apostles that this was his last supper until they met again in the kingdom of God.

How do we know that the bread and wine have become the sacred Body and Blood of Christ?

Through the Power of His Spirit

In a wonderful way Christ is present in the sacred bread we eat and the sacred wine we drink. In the celebration of the Eucharist, Christ is with us through the power of the Holy Spirit.

Throughout the entire Mass, we are gathered and led by God's Spirit. In the Eucharistic Prayer we ask the Father to send the Spirit. The Holy Spirit is called upon to bless the bread and wine and make them an acceptable sacrifice to God. Through the power of the Spirit, the bread and wine are completely changed. They are **consecrated**, transformed into something sacred. They become the Body and Blood of our Lord Jesus Christ. The Eucharistic Prayer is the prayer through which the community offers thanksgiving to God for salvation in Christ.

We, too, can be transformed in the Sacrament of the Eucharist. If we truly believe and respond in faith to the sacrament, we can be completely changed by the consecrated bread and wine. In Holy Communion we are joined in the Body and Blood of Christ. Jesus said, "Whoever eats my flesh and drinks my blood abides in me and I in him" *(John 6:56)*. Through the Eucharist we live in Christ, and Christ lives in us.

- **How do you think we are changed by the Eucharist?**

Our Moral Guide

The whole Christ is truly, really, and fully present in the Eucharist. The real presence of Christ among us in the Eucharist reminds us how Jesus loved us and gave himself up so that we might live.

Catechism, #1380

What does the real presence of Christ in the Eucharist move us to do?

This chart shows the movement of the Mass from the beginning of the Liturgy of the Eucharist through the dismissal.

The Liturgy of the Eucharist

Preparation of Gifts	*The Eucharistic Prayer*
• **Presentation of the Gifts** We bring our gifts of bread and wine to the altar. We offer ourselves to God. We share our material gifts with the community. During the procession we sing a hymn or pray an antiphon. • **Preparation of the Bread and Wine** The presider prays over the bread and wine, blessing God. He uses words similar to those used in the Jewish Sabbath blessings. The presider then invites us to join with him and with Jesus, our high priest, as we offer our sacrifice to God. • **Prayer over the Gifts** The presider, speaking for the gathered community, prays in words that express the theme of the celebration.	• **Preface** The presider begins the Eucharistic Prayer by recalling, in the presence of the assembly, God's wonderful kindness. • **Acclamation (Holy, Holy, Holy Lord)** We respond with a joyful song of praise. The words come from scriptural songs of praise sung by the angels and by those who welcomed Jesus into Jerusalem. • **Eucharistic Prayer** This great prayer is at the heart of our celebration. The presider first calls on the Holy Spirit to make us and our gifts worthy to be offered to God. Then, taking the place of Jesus, the presider consecrates the bread and wine. He uses Jesus' own words from the Last Supper. The bread and wine become Jesus. We proclaim our belief in the Paschal mystery by singing an acclamation. Then the presider recalls God's wonderful actions in raising Jesus to new life and saving us. He joins our prayers with those of all members of the Church, on earth and in heaven. We offer Jesus, and ourselves joined to Jesus, to the Father as the Eucharistic Prayer concludes with a *doxology*, or praise of the Trinity. We respond with a great "Amen"—"It is so!"

Communion Rite

- **The Lord's Prayer**

In the words Jesus gave us, we pray for the coming of God's kingdom.

- **The Breaking of the Bread**

The presider and deacon break the one loaf or large host into pieces. During the breaking of the bread, we pray or sing an ancient hymn to Jesus, the Lamb of God, who takes away our sins. We recall our own unworthiness to attend the heavenly banquet and we ask Jesus to heal us.

- **Holy Communion**

The presider and Eucharistic ministers distribute the Body and Blood of Christ to the assembly. We approach the table of the Lord to be nourished with his sacred Body and Blood. Just as bread feeds our bodies, so the Body and Blood of Christ feed our spirits. The Eucharist helps us grow in Christian life. During Communion we sing hymns or antiphons.

- **Song of Praise or Silent Reflection**

After communion we pray in quiet thanksgiving. Sometimes a meditation song is sung.

- **Prayer after Communion**

The presider, speaking for us, thanks God for sharing Jesus with us.

Concluding Rite

- **Greeting**

The presider begins the concluding rite with "The Lord be with you."

- **Blessing**

The presider blesses us in the name of the Father, and of the Son, and of the Holy Spirit.

- **Dismissal**

The presider or deacon sends us out from the Eucharistic assembly to love and serve the Lord in our daily lives. We respond "Thanks be to God."

- **Closing Song**

The presider and other liturgical ministers exit in procession. This action is often accompanied by the singing of a hymn.

RECALL

What happens when the priest consecrates the bread and wine? What prayer is most important and the heart of the Liturgy of the Eucharist?

THINK AND SHARE

How do you think the apostles felt when Jesus offered them sacred bread and wine in the way that he did?

CONTINUE THE JOURNEY

Write or draw one way in which the Eucharist changes you, as the bread and wine are changed.

Before

After

WE LIVE OUR FAITH

At Home With your family, make your favorite kind of bread or shop for a new variety. When you share the bread, thank God for the gift of Jesus in the Eucharist.

In the Parish Work with your classmates, your teacher or catechist, and your parish priest to plan a class Mass.

Truly Present

After Mass any remaining consecrated bread is placed in a special, decorated chest called a tabernacle. The word *tabernacle* means "meeting place." Jesus is truly present in the Eucharistic bread, known as the **Blessed Sacrament**. In many parishes the tabernacle is located in a separate chapel or area suitable for small-group prayer. A candle or lamp is kept burning to indicate that Jesus is present in the Blessed Sacrament.

Here is an ancient prayer honoring Jesus present in the Blessed Sacrament.

PRAYER

**Soul of Christ, sanctify us.
Body of Christ, save us.
Passion of Christ, strengthen us.
O good Jesus, hear us.
Never let us be separated from you.
Defend us from all harm.
At the hour of death, call us to your side,
that we may live forever with your saints,
praising you for all eternity.**

Review

Multiple Choice   Write the letter of the choice that best completes the sentence.

b 1. Bishops, priests, and deacons are called to special service in the Eucharistic assembly as **(a)** cantors **(b)** ordained ministers **(c)** altar servers **(d)** lectors.

_____ 2. We listen and respond to Scripture readings during the **(a)** Preface **(b)** Profession of Faith **(c)** Liturgy of the Word **(d)** Liturgy of the Eucharist.

_____ 3. At Mass Jesus is present in **(a)** the words and actions of the presider **(b)** the assembly **(c)** the Word of God **(d)** all of these.

_____ 4. When the bread and wine are consecrated, they become **(a)** Jesus, truly present **(b)** unchanged **(c)** invisible **(d)** too holy for us to eat.

_____ 5. The two major movements of the Eucharistic celebration are **(a)** the Presentation of the Gifts and Communion **(b)** the Body and Blood of Christ **(c)** the Liturgy of the Word and the Liturgy of the Eucharist **(d)** introductory and concluding rites.

Fill in the Blanks   Complete each sentence with the correct term.

1. The Christian Bible includes both the Old _____ and the New _____ .

2. We have an _____ to honor God by participating in the Eucharist each Sunday and holy day.

3. The book of Scripture readings arranged for use in the liturgy is called the _____ .

4. A _____ psalm follows the first reading at Mass.

5. The heart of the Liturgy of the Eucharist is the _____ Prayer.

Share Your Faith   Your friend invites you over on Sunday, but you are going to Mass. How would you explain to your friend why you will not cancel your plans to go to Mass?

Show How Far You've Come
Use this chart to show what you have learned. For each chapter, write the three most important things you remember.

The Eucharist, Our Great Sacrament

Chapter 21 Gathered Around the Altar	Chapter 22 God's Word Lives	Chapter 23 We Celebrate the Eucharist

What Else Would You Like to Know?

List any questions you still have about the importance of the Sacrament of the Eucharist.

_____

_____

_____

Continue the Journey
Choose one or more of the following activities to do on your own, with your class, or with your family.

- Look through your Faith Journal pages for Unit Six. Choose your favorite activity and share it with a friend or family member.

- Listen carefully to the Scripture readings at the Mass. In a notebook, copy passages from the Old Testament and New Testament that contain messages you especially want to remember.

- Discover ways you can increase your participation in the Eucharist. Find out how you can honor the Eucharist outside the celebration on Sunday.

Christ's Passover

PRAYER

Jesus, bring us together as one around the altar as we remember and participate in the mystery of our salvation.

Imagine yourself being plunged into a deep pool of water three times. With each plunge you enter more deeply into a dark, watery mystery. Afterward, you never look at water in quite the same way. You realize that it has the power both to give life and to take it away.

In a similar way the whole Church plunges into the mystery of Christ's dying and rising in the rituals of Holy Thursday, Good Friday, and Holy Saturday. These days are known as the *Triduum,* from the Latin word for "three days." They occur in Holy Week. Each sacred day reminds us of how we passed over from death to new life at our Baptism. Our passing from death to life is a sign of God's **covenant,** or sacred bond, with us. Just as the old covenant was sealed with the sacrifice at Mount Sinai, so the new covenant was sealed with Christ's offering of himself on the cross. Christ's death is the sacrifice of this covenant. Jesus passed through and overcame sin and death for us, rising to new life. We share in his dying and rising.

ACTIVITY

In your Bible, read the story of how God led the people of Israel safely through the sea *(Exodus 14:15—15:1).* With a partner, talk about why you think the Church uses this reading during Holy Week.

Our Bond with God Through Christ

The Mass of the Lord's Supper on Holy Thursday is our first plunge into the mystery of our salvation during Holy Week. It is a celebration of the new covenant, our sacred bond with God through Christ. In the Eucharist Christ offers the blood of the covenant. The first Eucharist anticipated that he would shed his blood for the forgiveness of sins *(Luke 22:19; Matthew 26:28)*. In the Eucharist we are brought back to God through the blood of Christ's sacrifice on the cross.

With the gift of the Holy Eucharist, Jesus showed us how to love. His love was so great that he gave himself completely for the life of the world. In another special action in his last days, Jesus showed us not only how to love but also how to serve one another. He washed the feet of his apostles. We remember these actions and their meaning in the Sacrament

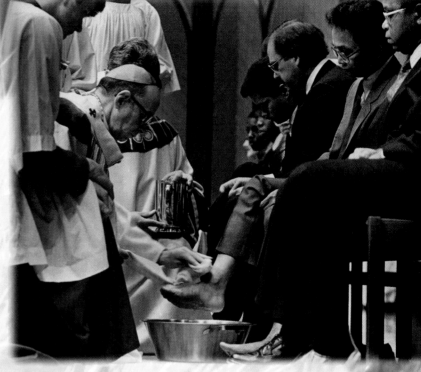

of the Eucharist and the ritual of foot washing on Holy Thursday.

As we pass through this life together, God is always washing us, feeding us, and healing us in the sacraments. The Holy Thursday ceremonies help us remember how blessed we are. We have been given the Eucharist with the command, "Do this in memory of me." Before he passed over from this world and returned to his Father, Jesus showed us the way with these words: "This I command you: love one another" *(John 15:17)*. God has loved us first in Christ. Our work is to show others the love and service Jesus showed so many.

On Holy Thursday Jesus' action of washing his friends' feet is symbolically enacted in churches all around the world.

Catholics Believe . . .

that Jesus offered the Eucharist as a memorial of his sacrifice and a sign of the new covenant between us and God.

Catechism, #611, 613

RECALL

What do we celebrate on Holy Thursday? What sacrament and ritual are part of Holy Thursday celebrations?

THINK AND SHARE

How, in our daily lives, can we follow Jesus' example in washing his friends' feet?

CONTINUE THE JOURNEY

Tell what each day of the Holy Week Triduum means to you.

Holy Thursday

_____

_____

_____

_____

_____

_____

_____

_____

Good Friday

_____

_____

_____

_____

_____

_____

_____

_____

_____

_____

_____

Holy Saturday

_____

_____

_____

_____

_____

_____

_____

_____

WE LIVE OUR FAITH

At Home Think of ways you can show kindness to members of your family and accept kindness from them. Remember that kindnesses may be acts of love or service. Begin practicing your ideas during Holy Week.

In the Parish Attend Holy Thursday ceremonies in your parish. During the Eucharist, pray for your parish priests. Remember that they have been ordained to serve as ministers, preaching the word and celebrating the sacraments for the entire Church.

Saint Thomas's Song

Thomas Aquinas is considered one of the finest writers in the history of the Church. But he began his life as a tongue-tied, clumsy student. His classmates teased Thomas by calling him "the dumb ox." Thomas's teacher, Saint Albert the Great, knew that Thomas had talent. "One day," he said, "the 'dumb ox' will sing a song heard all around the world."

Saint Albert was right. Thomas wrote many books about God. He also wrote a hymn in honor of the Eucharist that is still sung today. At the end of the Mass of the Lord's Supper on Holy Thursday, the words of Thomas's song echo around the world.

Sing or pray these words from Thomas's song together.

PRAYER

On the night of that Last Supper,
Seated with his chosen band,
He, the paschal victim eating,
First fulfills the law's command;
Then as food to all his brethren
Gives himself with his own hand.

Word made Flesh, the bread of nature,
By his word to flesh he turns;
Wine into his blood he changes:
What though sense no change discerns,
Only be the heart in earnest,
Faith her lesson quickly learns.

To the everlasting Father,
And the Son who reigns on high
With the Holy Spirit proceeding
Forth from each eternally,
Be salvation, honor, blessing,
Might and endless majesty.

CHAPTER 25

Celebrating Our Jewish Roots

PRAYER

May the God of Abraham and Sarah, Isaac and Jacob, and Jesus the Christ bless us. Help us see that we, Jews and Christians, have been chosen by God to reveal God's glory.

An old Jewish teacher, or *rabbi,* was visited by an *abbot* whose monastery was in decline. All the monks in the monastery were more than 70 years old. The abbot asked the rabbi for advice. The wise old teacher responded, "One of you might be the Messiah." The abbot was both comforted and disturbed by what the rabbi had said. He returned to the monastery and repeated the rabbi's words to his aging brothers. From that day forward something wonderful happened in the monastery. Each brother began to see every other monk as the Messiah in disguise. Word spread of the monks' love for one another. Many young men wanted to join their ranks. Thanks to the rabbi's gift, the monastery was revived, like a desert that had been watered.

ACTIVITY

List the similarities you see between the worship of the Jewish people and our own worship.

Bonds of Faith

Christians have received many gifts from their Jewish ancestors. Jesus is the greatest of these gifts. He was born of Mary of Nazareth and was raised by her and her husband, Joseph, of the House of David. We believe that Jesus was the Messiah that God promised to the people of Israel. Coming to us in the flesh, Jesus is the fulfillment of God's promises.

Although some Jewish people today still await a messiah, Catholics and Jews have much in common. We share the Ten Commandments, the gift of God's law and holy will. Jews and Christians alike observe the commandments in a covenant with God that is based on love. We also share Scripture, the sacred writings in which the commandments are recorded. The word of God in the Old Testament forms part of public worship for both Jews and Christians. When we worship, we pray the psalms, prayers in the Old Testament composed by the inspired poets of Israel. When we speak out against violence or unjust acts, we often turn to the words of the Hebrew prophets. Commandments, covenant, Scripture, and worship are our bonds of faith with the Jewish people.

Scripture Signpost

"They are Israelites; theirs the adoption, the glory, the covenants, the giving of the law, the worship, and the promises; theirs the patriarchs, and from them, according to the flesh, is the Messiah."
Romans 9:4–5

What have the Jewish people contributed to our faith?

From the moment of their Exodus from Egypt, the Israelites became God's chosen people, and God became their one God.

Catholics Believe . . .

that we share a belief in one God, Scripture, ways of worship, and prayers with the Jewish people.

Catechism, #1096

The Passover

The story of creation in Genesis, the first book of the Old Testament, tells us that the Spirit of God passed over the waters, and they stirred with life (*Genesis 1:20–21*). In Exodus, the second book, God passed over the houses of a group of slaves and spared them from the angel of death. Then God led these people, the Israelites, out of Egypt, and they passed over into freedom (*Exodus 12–14*). To mark the event of their passing over, God commanded the Israelite community to celebrate a sacred meal.

The Jews are the descendants of the Israelites, whom God led out of Egypt. To this day Jews all over the world celebrate Passover with a special evening meal called the **Seder**. The **Exodus**, or departure, of the Israelites from Egypt is the focus of the Seder. At the meal the story of the Exodus is retold and experienced by those gathered. The story is told not as a past event but as if it were happening now.

During the meal the youngest child asks why the night is different from all others. In answer to the question, an older, respected member of the household tells about the Exodus. The storyteller explains how God passed over the houses of the chosen people and led the Israelites as they passed over from slavery to freedom. Special foods eaten in a certain order help those gathered remember the events of the Passover.

Words and actions draw those sitting at the table into the story of God's mighty deeds. Nothing so great had ever happened before; no such thing had ever been heard of (*Deuteronomy 4:32*). The story of the Exodus recalls what God did and continues to do for the Jewish people and all who believe, then and now. With the Jews we turn to the one and only God, who was first revealed to them. With them we love the Lord our God with all our heart, with all our soul, and with all our strength (*Deuteronomy 6:5*). We proclaim as one, "Praise be to the Lord, the King of the Universe."

ACTIVITY

Draw a picture of a religious celebration that brings your family together. Explain to your classmates the parts of the celebration your picture shows.

Anti-Semitism is any form of hatred directed toward the Jewish people. We need to oppose any word or action that attacks the dignity of the Jews, whose heritage of faith we share.

Catechism, #839

What can we do to fight anti-Semitism?

Renewing Ties

Christians share a rich heritage of faith with the Jewish people. Yet in spite of this, Jews through the ages have suffered terribly at the hands of Christians. Not long after the followers of Jesus parted ways with the Jews, suspicions arose and insults were traded between the two communities.

Over time, as Christianity became the favored religion in the Roman Empire, some Christians developed strong feelings of hatred toward the Jews. Irresponsible but powerful Christians focused on Jewish people whenever they needed someone to blame, someone to be a *scapegoat*. Horrible crimes were committed against the Jews, including the *Shoah*, or Holocaust, in the twentieth century. In the 1930s and 1940s, Jews in Germany and across Europe were persecuted and killed by the millions.

We must remember these terrible actions against the Jewish people. We must repent and resolve never to let such hatred and crimes happen again. As we explore the mystery of our own faith, we discover our close connections with the Jewish people. Through prayer and sincere actions, we can strengthen the special link between Jews and Christians. We can be enriched by what we share with other people of faith.

In 1986 Pope John Paul II made history by meeting with the chief rabbi of Rome at the Rome Synagogue.

Major Feasts Celebrated by the Jewish Community

Rosh Hashanah

The Jewish New Year, celebrating God as Creator and King of the Universe

Yom Kippur

Day of atonement, or reconciliation with God, the holiest day of the year among Jews, marked by prayer and fasting

Shavu'ot

(also known as Feast of Weeks or Pentecost)

Feast observed 50 days after Passover to mark the giving of the Law to Moses

Sukkot

(also known as Feast of Booths or Tabernacles)

Nine-day harvest festival celebrating God's blessings in the past, present, and future and remembering the shelters used by Jews as they wandered in the wilderness

Passover

Seven-day celebration of the Israelites' freedom from slavery and the Exodus from Egypt

Hanukkah

Eight-day festival of lights, recalling how freedom to worship God was restored to the Jews after the Temple at Jerusalem was destroyed by nonbelievers and then rededicated

RECALL

With what group do we share a heritage of faith? What event does the Jewish holiday of Passover mark? What is the Seder?

THINK AND SHARE

Why do you think we should reach out to people of other faiths?

CONTINUE THE JOURNEY

Write a letter to a Jewish boy or girl your age. Describe what you have in common. Then tell what you would like to learn about the Jewish faith. Also say what you would like to share about your own faith.

WE LIVE OUR FAITH

At Home   Make an effort to get to know young people of other faiths who live in your neighborhood. Introduce your new friends to your family.

In the Parish   Find out if you and your classmates might be able to take part in a Seder. Ask a parish staff member for help in making arrangements.

Sing to the Lord

When Moses and the Israelites came to the Red Sea, God divided the waters so that they could cross on dry land between two great walls of water. The sea then flowed back to wash away the Egyptians pursuing them. After safely crossing the Red Sea, the Israelites sang a song of praise to God. Miriam, Moses' sister, led the celebration with dancing accompanied by tambourines. The song the people of Israel sang has become part of Christian liturgy for the Easter Vigil, celebrating God's saving power.

Prayer

Select one person to recite Exodus 15:1–18, the song that Moses and the Israelites sang after crossing the Red Sea. After each verse, respond as a group with the refrain that Miriam sang:

Sing to the Lord, for he is gloriously triumphant; horse and chariot he has cast into the sea.

—Exodus 15:21

CHAPTER 26

Death and Resurrection

PRAYER

Lord Jesus, you suffered death on a cross to bring new life to the world. Be with us now and at the hour of our death so that we may rise to new life in your resurrection.

Dear God,

I feel so alone. It seems as if my whole life changed overnight. Last night my best friend died in a car crash. I don't understand. Why her? She was young just like me, and now she's gone. All I have left is an ache in my heart that won't go away.

I believe she is with you now in heaven. That's what Jesus promised to anyone who had faith in his words. It's so hard to hold on to that hope, though. I feel sad and angry at the same time. Please help me put my trust in you now more than ever.

Love,

T. J.

Like the person who wrote this letter, we are stunned and confused when someone we love dies. We ask questions that are difficult to answer: Why him? Why her? Why not me? Why now? What does it all mean? What is the meaning of life? We are reminded of how fragile life is. We see what a gift life is and how we sometimes take it for granted.

We react to death in many ways. We may fall to our knees and pray, or our anger may keep us away from prayer altogether. Death is not a time to turn away, however. Instead, we need to turn toward life, to those around us and above all to God, who is the source of all life. Answers to our questions may not come easily. Yet we can find comfort and support in the promise and hope that God, who raised Jesus from the dead, will also raise us to life everlasting.

Scripture Signpost

"I am the resurrection and the life; whoever believes in me, even if he dies, will live, and everyone who lives and believes in me will never die. Do you believe this?"

John 11:25–26

Who is speaking? To whom is the question addressed? Why is the question important?

ACTIVITY

Write a letter to comfort a friend who has lost a loved one.

Catholics Believe . . .

that at death we are led to the kingdom of God and new life in Christ, a journey we began at Baptism.

Catechism, #1682

SCRIPTURE STORY

Our Faith Is Not in Vain!

Strange as it may seem, some early Christians began to declare that the dead would not be resurrected. Others said that those who were alive were already risen. With no life in the future to believe in, they started to live by the motto "Let us eat and drink, for tomorrow we die."

The news of the views of these Christians reached the apostle Paul. He did not hesitate to tell them that they were completely wrong. Paul used reason and logic to prove their views wrong, point by point. If there is no resurrection of the dead, he observed, then Christ has not been raised. If Christ has not been raised, then Paul's own preaching and that of the other apostles is empty. If Christ has not been raised, Paul went on, then Christian faith is in vain. It has no use or worth. Without faith, without belief in the risen Christ, there is no forgiveness of sins and no salvation. But people still have their sins. Therefore, those who died believing in the risen Christ are lost forever.

Paul's argument was clear and convincing, but he was not quite finished. To stress the nonsense of such views, he remarked:

> "If for this life only we have hoped in Christ, we are the most pitiable people of all. . . . But thanks be to God who gives us victory through our Lord Jesus Christ."

—based on 1 Corinthians 15:12–19, 32, 57

ACTIVITY

Draw two pictures, one next to the other. First, draw a seed buried in the earth. Then, draw the same seed springing forth from the earth in new life.

We Believe in Life Now and Forever

Because Jesus chose to become one of us and lived and died among us, our life now has a new and deeper meaning. Because Jesus died for us and rose to new life, death is not our final end. Jesus' passover, or passing over, from death to new life is a mystery in which we can share through the sacramental life of his Church. The mystery of dying in order to live unfolds in the celebration of the sacraments. With Baptism we begin the process of dying to our old selves in order to live for our new selves in Christ.

Jesus ascended to his Father. He will come again in glory to bring God's kingdom in fullness.

The Easter candle and the pall are reminders of Baptism, through which we are reborn in Christ.

The Journey Home

Throughout our lives the Church encourages us to prepare for the time of our death, when we will be led to new life in the kingdom of God. The **last rites** are part of our preparation as we draw near to death and are about to make the final journey home to God. In the last rites we pray, celebrate the Sacraments of Reconciliation and Anointing, and receive the Eucharist a last time. This last Eucharist is offered to us as **viaticum**, Latin for "food for the journey." It will help us pass over from death to life, from the world on earth to God, from sin to grace.

After a person has died, the Church celebrates a Mass of Christian Burial. Funerals are part of the liturgy of the Church. One purpose of a funeral is to bring the community of the Church together and proclaim the message of eternal life. Another is to pray for eternal life for the one who has died.

At the Mass of Christian Burial, the coffin containing the body of the person who has died is met by the presider at the church entrance. The presider blesses the coffin with holy water. The lighted Easter candle reminds those gathered of the person's dying and rising in Christ. The **pall**, a white cloth like the white garment received in Baptism, is draped over the coffin.

The Scripture readings during the Liturgy of the Word focus on God's constant mercy and forgiveness. In the homily words of *consolation,* or comfort, based on the Paschal mystery are offered to those gathered. In the general intercessions family members join their prayers for the dead with the prayers of the whole Body of Christ.

During the Liturgy of the Eucharist, the Church names and prays for the person who has died. The Church asks that the person be admitted to the kingdom of God. As those present gather around the table of the Eucharist, they remember the sacrifice of Jesus' death and the glory of his resurrection.

In the final farewell before the body is buried, the Church *commends,* or gives, the person who has died to God. The person is also commended into the care of Mary and the saints. Then the Church calls upon choirs of angels to welcome the person into the paradise of God's heavenly kingdom. There every tear will be wiped away, and one day all the faithful will be together in Christ.

There is sorrow in death, but there is also hope because of the death and resurrection of Christ.

RECALL

Why do we believe that death is not our final end? What do the last rites include? What is viaticum?

THINK AND SHARE

How do you think the Mass of Christian Burial helps those who have suffered the loss of a loved one?

CONTINUE THE JOURNEY

Make a prayer card. Write the words from John 11:25–26 on the card: "I am the resurrection and the life; whoever believes in me, even if he dies, will live, and everyone who lives and believes in me will never die." Turn to the card for comfort at times when you remember those who have gone before you in hope of the resurrection.

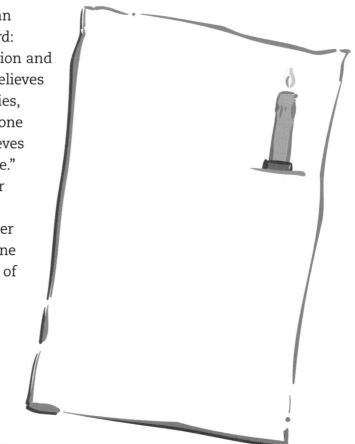

WE LIVE OUR FAITH

 At Home At bedtime, remember and pray for members of your family who have died.

In the Parish During the general intercessions at Mass, listen carefully for the names of people in the Church community who have died during the past week. Pray for them.

For Those Who Mourn

We have a duty to pray for those who have died. But we pray, too, for their relatives and friends. Sorrow does not slip away easily after someone dies. Those who are left behind need the prayers and care of others in the community of faith.

As you pray this prayer together, call to mind people you know who need comfort as they mourn and grieve for those who have died.

PRAYER

Lord God,
you are attentive to the voice of
    our pleading.
Let us find in your Son
comfort in our sadness,
certainty in our doubt,
and courage to live through
    this hour.
Make our faith strong
through Christ our Lord. Amen.

—from the Order of
Christian Funerals

CHAPTER 27

The Life of the World to Come

PRAYER

God, help us serve your kingdom now so that we may rejoice in its fullness and glory forever.

"I give up!" David yelled. "I've been trying to play this stupid thing for weeks, and all I get is squeaking! I'll never be able to make music."

David glared at his clarinet as though it were a monster. Every time he thought he could get through a song, his fingers got tangled or he ran out of breath. He couldn't get the music he heard in his head to come out of the clarinet.

"Don't worry, David," said Mrs. Schaefer, his music teacher. "It's always this way at the beginning. Just be patient and keep practicing. And don't give up! Listen . . . "

Mrs. Schaefer played a recording. The clarinet solo rose up out of the orchestra with every note clear and beautiful. "David," Mrs. Schaefer said, "I promise you that if you keep working, one day this will be you."

A Powerful Pull

We are all beginners when it comes to working for the kingdom of God now and waiting for its final coming in glory. In our everyday lives we are involved in the tug-of-war between what is and what should be. Grace pulls us toward God's **reign**, or kingdom. Sin pulls us away. We live in tension and constant pulling.

Yet we are not like the three monkeys who saw, heard, and spoke no evil. We do see, hear, and speak of the evil and suffering that are around us. We work earnestly to make the world a better place to live. Our real efforts in the present allow us to look forward to a new heaven and a new earth in the future. We work now, knowing that God's promise of salvation has already been fulfilled in Christ Jesus, the "firstborn of this creation" (*Colossians* 1:15). We have a reason to hope and to keep walking in faith.

ACTIVITY

Make a list of several people you can turn to when you have serious questions about living the Christian life.

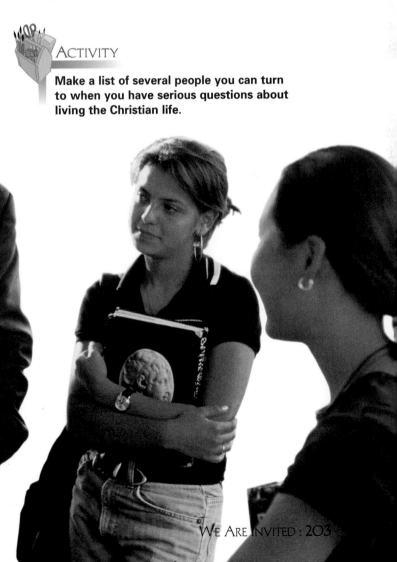

What do you think the new Jerusalem represents? What are its riches meant to show?

SCRIPTURE STORY
A Heavenly Vision

Catholics Believe . . .

that God's kingdom is the reign of justice, love, and peace.

Catechism, #672

God sent a series of visions to a man named John. One was a vision of the new creation, God's reign fulfilled. John saw a new heaven and a new earth. He also saw the holy city, the new Jerusalem, coming down out of heaven.

The city of John's vision sparkled. The foundations of the wall that surrounded it were decorated with every precious stone. Its towering wall had twelve gates of priceless pearls, which were guarded by twelve angels of the Lord. The holy city's main street was made of pure gold, transparent as glass. There was no temple in the city, for no temple was needed. The Lord God almighty and Jesus, the Lamb of God, had become the perfect temple.

The entire city was lit by the brightness of God's glory. It needed no sun or moon to light its day or night. Its light would show the way for nations and would never go out. Its gates would always be open to all people of goodwill. Peoples from every nation would pass through the gates, bringing gifts and treasures to place before the throne of God. The names of those who entered would be written in the Book of Life.

—based on Revelation 21:9–26

Working Toward the Vision

Before the new, heavenly city of Jerusalem comes in its fullness, we have work to do here and now. Many people on earth are hungry and thirsty. Many live without proper clothing or shelter. Others are sick or trapped in desperate situations. Our own cities definitely do not have streets of gold and gates of pearl.

In the celebration of Christ's sacraments, especially the Eucharist, we are blessed and nourished so that we can share our blessings with others. We can fill their needs in Jesus' name. To feed the hungry, give drink to the thirsty, clothe the naked, shelter the homeless, visit the sick and the imprisoned—these are our Works of Mercy. The day will come when God "will wipe every tear from their eyes, and there shall be no more death or mourning, wailing or pain" (*Revelation 21:4*). Until that day, however, all Christians have a responsibility to work for justice and peace. What we do for the least of God's people is important now in this life. And it will be important when Christ returns in glory.

Scripture Signpost

"I also saw the holy city, a new Jerusalem, coming down out of heaven from God. . . ."
Revelation 21:2

Who will be welcomed into the new Jerusalem?

ACTIVITY

Discuss the steps you would take to organize a service project that will work for justice or peace in your community.

This tapestry shows how Jesus used words and signs to invite us into God's kingdom. The left side shows the Sermon on the Mount. On the right Jesus heals a leper as a sign of God's transforming love.

We Are Invited

Our invitation to feast in God's kingdom began with the signs and wonders of creation. Out of love God created man and woman and gave them a garden filled with every kind of tree "delightful to look at and good for food" (*Genesis 2:9*). But the first humans turned away from God, and sin and evil entered the world. God did not turn away from us, however. God kept sending us signs of hope and promise, especially through the people of Israel. If they remained faithful, God promised, they would enter a land flowing with milk and honey. All the nations of the earth would rejoice with them in a great feast.

Then Jesus came among us. He used parables to teach us about God's reign. Jesus showed us that the kingdom was for all people, the Jewish people and all others. Through words and actions he invited everyone into the kingdom of God. He also showed us that the kingdom is among us. At a special meal with his closest friends, he blessed bread and wine and changed them into his own Body and Blood. The gift Jesus gave of himself that night became our sacrament of life-giving Bread and saving Cup. Jesus commanded us to celebrate the Eucharistic feast until he comes again in glory.

The Kingdom in Glory

We celebrate the sacraments as constant reminders that God's reign is among us. Each sacrament also points to the future when the kingdom will be fulfilled in glory. When Christ returns at the end of time and hands the kingdom over to his Father, there will be no need for signs and sacraments. At the heavenly banquet we will see and be seen without images and symbols. In the words of Saint Paul:

> At present we see indistinctly, as in a mirror, but then face to face. At present I know partially; then I shall know fully as I am fully known. So faith, hope, love remain, these three; but the greatest of these is love.
>
> —1 Corinthians 13:12–13

Like all those on a journey, we need to keep our feet on the ground and our eyes on the stars. We must also remember that we do not travel alone. We are pilgrims who walk together by faith. Our hope is in God's promise of salvation and the life of the world to come. In this world right now, while we wait, we must serve God by loving one another.

ACTIVITY

We travel toward God together. Draw a picture of what you imagine the heavenly banquet in God's reign will be like.

RECALL

What is another way of describing God's kingdom? What must we do to be in God's kingdom? Why do we celebrate the sacraments?

THINK AND SHARE

What are some signs of God's kingdom among us?

CONTINUE THE JOURNEY

Draw or write about the one event you will most remember from your faith journey this year.

WE LIVE OUR FAITH

 At Home Pray the Lord's Prayer at your bedside or with members of your family. Reflect on the words "your kingdom come."

In the Parish Participate as fully as possible in the next celebration of the Eucharist. Approach the Eucharist as a joyous occasion that is a sign that the kingdom of God is alive and active in your parish.

A Joyful Jubilee

Somber notes and a solemn shuffle are all that are heard when a funeral procession starts off through the streets of New Orleans. Then, unexpectedly, there is a trumpet blast, and the whole band strikes up a *jubilee*, or shout of joy: "When the Saints Go Marchin' In." Everyone joins in the joyous song as the band dances its way up the street.

Look forward in prayer to the kingdom that will be fulfilled in glory. Close your prayer by singing "When the Saints Go Marchin' In."

PRAYER

At the heavenly banquet in the new Jerusalem, Jesus the Lamb of God will spread a table and feed us.

He is our Beginning and End. Then we shall come to know God in a vision so blessed that we will know as we are known.

Amen. Alleluia!

Review

Matching
Match the meanings in Column A with the correct terms in Column B.

Column A

_____ 1. Departure of the Israelites from Egypt.

_____ 2. Any form of hatred directed toward the Jewish people.

_____ 3. Responsibility of all Christians.

_____ 4. Sacred meal to celebrate Passover.

_____ 5. Kingdom.

Column B

a. anti-Semitism

b. Seder

c. Exodus

d. reign

e. working for justice

Multiple Choice
Write the letter of the choice that best completes the sentence.

_____ 1. Jesus is the greatest of all the gifts we have received from the (a) Bible (b) Jewish people (c) Church (d) covenant.

_____ 2. Because Jesus died for us and rose to new life, death is (a) something we fear (b) not hard for us (c) not our final end (d) a time of sorrow.

_____ 3. The last Eucharist we receive is called *viaticum*, or (a) farewell (b) food for the journey (c) Reconciliation (d) funeral.

_____ 4. Justice, love, mercy, and peace are signs of (a) the end of time (b) death (c) mourning (d) God's reign.

_____ 5. With the Jewish people we share commandments, covenant, Scripture, and (a) sacraments (b) the pope (c) ways of worship (d) Christmas.

Share Your Faith
You hear someone say that we might as well enjoy ourselves now because this life is all we have. Explain why you believe in new life beyond death.

Show How Far You've Come

Use this chart to show what you have learned. For each chapter, write the three most important things you remember.

The Paschal Mystery

Chapter 25 Celebrating Our Jewish Roots	Chapter 26 Death and Resurrection	Chapter 27 The Life of the World to Come

What Else Would You Like to Know?

List any questions you still have about the history of our salvation.

_____

_____

_____

Continue the Journey

Choose one or more of the following activities to do on your own, with your class, or with your family.

- Look through your Faith Journal pages for Unit Seven. Choose your favorite activity and share it with a friend or family member.

- Explore further our bonds of faith with the Jewish people. Ask a parish staff member if it might be possible to organize a discussion group of young Jews and Christians. Decide on topics of discussion together. Share ideas. Enjoy what you have in common and how you differ from each other.

- List ways you can serve God's kingdom right now. Start small and close to home. Try out your ideas right away. Make good works part of your life.

The Great

PRAYER

God, your love and mercy know no limits in bringing salvation to all people. Show your saving power this night in the mystery of the risen Christ.

Tonight, fire, candle, Christ is our Light. The night watch is over, our Savior is risen, Christians the world over freed from death's prison.

Tonight, story of salvation, from the beginning. How God, stretching out hand and mighty arm, To the promised land led the chosen unharmed.

Tonight, promises made, renewed, in baptismal waters. Together we celebrate that the risen One leads us And with holy bread and wine at table feeds us.

Tonight, sin is undone, and a new life begun. Let us shake the foundations with our song: "Alleluia, Alleluia! Christ, come!"

ACTIVITY

Study the poem about the Easter Vigil. Identify the parts of the Easter Vigil service the verses describe.

Vigil

A Year to Remember

The word *vigil* means "keeping watch by night." At the **Easter Vigil** on Holy Saturday evening, we keep watch at the tomb of Jesus, ready to greet him when he rises to new life. On this night of nights, those who have prepared to be initiated into the Church will join the community of faith. Newly baptized, they will go forth from the celebration to spread the good news of salvation. They will continue their journey into the Paschal mystery.

You, too, will continue your journey. This year you have been on a sacramental journey filled with signs and wonders. Along the way you have learned that God uses signs in many ways. Through signs God gives us grace, shows us love, and tells us about wonders we cannot see.

You have also opened yourself to God's word this year. You entered into the Scriptures through prayer and study. Each time you celebrated God's word was a sacramental moment. You will be reminded of this as you hear the stories you have come to know echoed in the readings of the Easter Vigil.

Like those coming into the Church on the night of the Vigil, you have learned about how Jesus gave us the sacraments, especially the Sacrament of the Eucharist. You know now that these seven sacred signs celebrate God's life within us.

At the Easter Vigil we give thanks and praise to God for Christ's victory over death in the resurrection. In Christ's dying and rising, we experience God's love. Here and now we live in faith and hope. In the kingdom of God, present and to come, we will live in God's love forever.

Catholics Believe . . .

that in the Easter Vigil the Church recalls and celebrates the great events of our salvation by God.

Catechism, #1217

Recall

What does the Easter Vigil celebrate?

Think and Share

Why do you think the Easter Vigil is such an important celebration among Christians?

Continue the Journey

Write a poem for Easter. In your poem, tell what the celebration of Easter means to you.

We Live Our Faith

At Home Create a card for your family that celebrates Christ's resurrection. Put the card in a noticeable place in your home so that everyone in your family will see it on Easter morning.

In the Parish If possible, attend your parish's Easter Vigil. Listen carefully to the readings to hear once again the story of our salvation.

We Have Come Full Circle

At the Easter Vigil we have the opportunity to renew our own baptismal promises with those who are about to celebrate their Baptism. Let us return to our beginning at the baptismal font and to the promises made to God on the holy day of our Baptism.

PRAYER

Respond together to the questions. Then recite the Nicene Creed or the Apostles' Creed.

Leader: Do you reject evil and renew your commitment to Jesus Christ?

All: I do.

Leader: Do you believe in God, the Father almighty, creator of heaven and earth?

All: I do.

Leader: Do you believe in Jesus Christ, Son of God?

All: I do.

Leader: Do you believe in the Holy Spirit?

All: I do.

Leader: Will you proclaim by word and example the good news of God in Christ?

All: I will, with God's help.

Leader: Will you strive for justice and peace among all people?

All: I will, with God's help.

CATHOLIC PRAYERS AND RESOURCES

The Sign of the Cross

In the name of the Father, and of the Son, and of the Holy Spirit.
Amen.

The Lord's Prayer

Traditional/Liturgical
Our Father,
  who art in heaven,
hallowed be thy name;
thy kingdom come;
thy will be done on earth
  as it is in heaven.
Give us this day our
  daily bread;
and forgive us our
  trespasses
as we forgive those who
  trespass against us;
and lead us not into
temptation,
but deliver us from evil.
(Amen.)
For the kingdom,
the power,
and the glory are yours,
now and for ever.

Contemporary
Our Father in heaven,
  hallowed be your name,
  your kingdom come,
  your will be done,
  on earth as in heaven.
Give us today our
  daily bread.
Forgive us our sins
  as we forgive those who
  sin against us.
Save us from the time
  of trial
  and deliver us from evil.
For the kingdom, the
  power, and the glory are
  yours, now and for ever.
Amen.

Scriptural
"Our Father in heaven,
hallowed be your name,
your kingdom come,
your will be done,
on earth as in heaven.
Give us today our daily
  bread;
and forgive us our debts
as we forgive our debtors;
and do not subject us to
  the final test,
but deliver us from the
  evil one."
       —Matthew 6:9–13
"Father, hallowed be
  your name,
  your kingdom come.
Give us each day our
  daily bread
and forgive us our sins
for we ourselves forgive
  everyone in debt
  to us,
and do not subject us to
  the final test."
       —Luke 11:2–4

Hail Mary

Hail, Mary, full of grace,
the Lord is with you!
Blessed are you among women,
and blessed is the fruit of your womb, Jesus.
Holy Mary, Mother of God,
pray for us sinners,
now and at the hour of our death.
Amen.

Glory to the Father *(Doxology)*

Glory to the Father, and to the Son, and to the Holy Spirit:
as it was in the beginning, is now, and will be for ever.
(Amen.)

Prayer to the Guardian Angel

Angel sent by God to guide me,
be my light and walk beside me;
be my guardian and protect me;
on the path of life direct me.

Morning Prayer

Almighty God,
you have given us this day:
strengthen us with your power
and keep us from falling into sin,
so that whatever we say or think or do
may be in your service and for the sake of your kingdom.
We ask this through Christ our Lord.
Amen.

Evening Prayer

Lord, watch over us this night.
By your strength, may we rise at daybreak
to rejoice in the resurrection of Christ, your Son,
who lives and reigns for ever.
Amen.

Blessing Before Meals

Bless us, O Lord, and these your gifts
which we are about to receive from your goodness.
Through Christ our Lord.
Amen.

Thanksgiving After Meals

We give you thanks for all your gifts, almighty God,
living and reigning now and for ever.
Amen.

The Apostles' Creed

I believe in God, the Father almighty,
    creator of heaven and earth.
I believe in Jesus Christ, his only Son,
    our Lord.
    He was conceived by the power of the
        Holy Spirit
        and born of the Virgin Mary.
    He suffered under Pontius Pilate,
        was crucified, died, and was buried.
    He descended to the dead.
    On the third day, he rose again.

He ascended into heaven,
        and is seated at the right hand
        of the Father.
    He will come again to judge the living
        and the dead.
I believe in the Holy Spirit,
    the holy catholic Church,
    the communion of saints,
    the forgiveness of sins,
    the resurrection of the body,
    and life everlasting. Amen.

The Nicene Creed

We believe in one God,
    the Father, the Almighty,
    maker of heaven and earth,
    of all that is, seen and unseen.
We believe in one Lord, Jesus Christ,
    the only Son of God,
    eternally begotten of the Father,
    God from God, Light from Light,
    true God from true God,
    begotten, not made, one in Being with
        the Father.
    Through him all things were made.
    For us men and for our salvation
        he came down from heaven:
    by the power of the Holy Spirit
        he was born of the Virgin Mary,
        and became man.
    For our sake he was crucified under
        Pontius Pilate;
    he suffered, died, and was buried.
    On the third day he rose again
        in fulfillment of the Scriptures;

he ascended into heaven
        and is seated at the right hand
            of the Father.
    He will come again in glory to judge
        the living and the dead,
        and his kingdom will have no end.
We believe in the Holy Spirit, the Lord,
    the giver of life,
    who proceeds from the Father
        and the Son.
    With the Father and the Son he is
        worshiped and glorified.
    He has spoken through the Prophets.
    We believe in one holy catholic and
        apostolic Church.
    We acknowledge one baptism for the
        forgiveness of sins.
    We look for the resurrection
        of the dead,
        and the life of the world to come.
    Amen.

Act of Faith

O God, we firmly believe that you are one God in three divine Persons, Father, Son, and Holy Spirit; we believe that your divine Son became man and died for our sins, and that he will come to judge the living and the dead. We believe these and all the truths that the holy Catholic Church teaches, because you have revealed them, and you can neither deceive nor be deceived.

Act of Hope

O God, relying on your almighty power and your endless mercy and promises, we hope to gain pardon for our sins, the help of your grace, and life everlasting, through the saving actions of Jesus Christ, our Lord and Redeemer.

Act of Love

O God, we love you above all things, with our whole heart and soul, because you are all-good and worthy of all love. We love our neighbor as ourselves for the love of you. We forgive all who have injured us and ask pardon of all whom we have injured.

Prayer to the Holy Spirit

Come, Holy Spirit, fill the hearts of your faithful.
And kindle in them the fire of your love.
Send forth your Spirit and they shall be created.
And you will renew the face of the earth.
Lord,
by the light of the Holy Spirit
you have taught the hearts of your faithful.
In the same Spirit
help us choose what is right
and always rejoice in your consolation.
We ask this through Christ our Lord.
Amen.

The Jesus Prayer

Lord Jesus Christ,
Son of God,
have mercy on me, a sinner.
Amen.

Act of Contrition

My God,
I am sorry for my sins with all my heart.
In choosing to do wrong
and failing to do good,
I have sinned against you
whom I should love above all things.
I firmly intend, with your help,
to do penance,
to sin no more,
and to avoid whatever leads me to sin.
Our Savior Jesus Christ
suffered and died for us.
In his name, my God, have mercy.

I Confess

I confess to almighty God,
and to you, my brothers and sisters,
that I have sinned through my own fault
in my thoughts and in my words,
in what I have done,
and in what I have failed to do;
and I ask blessed Mary, ever virgin,
all the angels and saints,
and you, my brothers and sisters,
to pray for me to the Lord our God.

The Books of the Bible

The Catholic *canon*, or authorized version, of the Bible contains 73 books—46 in the Old Testament and 27 in the New Testament.

The Old Testament

The Pentateuch
Genesis ✓
Exodus
Leviticus
Numbers
Deuteronomy

Joshua
Judges
Ruth

The Historical Books
1 Samuel
2 Samuel
1 Kings
2 Kings
1 Chronicles
2 Chronicles
Ezra
Nehemiah
Tobit
Judith
Esther
1 Maccabees
2 Maccabees

The Wisdom Books
Job
Psalms
Proverbs
Ecclesiastes
Song of Songs
Wisdom
Sirach (Ecclesiasticus)

The Prophetic Books
Isaiah
Jeremiah
Lamentations
Baruch
Ezekiel
Daniel
Hosea
Joel
Amos
Obadiah
Jonah
Micah
Nahum
Habakkuk
Zephaniah
Haggai
Zechariah
Malachi

The New Testament

The Gospels
Matthew
Mark
Luke
John

The Acts of the Apostles

The New Testament Letters
Romans
1 Corinthians
2 Corinthians
Galatians
Ephesians
Philippians
Colossians
1 Thessalonians
2 Thessalonians
1 Timothy
2 Timothy
Titus
Philemon
Hebrews

The Catholic Letters
James
1 Peter
2 Peter
1 John
2 John
3 John
Jude

The Book of Revelation

The Great Commandment

"You shall love the Lord your God with all your heart,
with all your soul, with all your strength, and with all your mind;
and your neighbor as yourself."

—Luke 10:27

The Ten Commandments

1. I am the Lord your God. You shall not have strange gods before me.
2. You shall not take the name of the Lord your God in vain.
3. Remember to keep holy the Lord's day.
4. Honor your father and your mother.
5. You shall not kill.
6. You shall not commit adultery.
7. You shall not steal.
8. You shall not bear false witness against your neighbor.
9. You shall not covet your neighbor's wife.
10. You shall not covet your neighbor's goods.

The Beatitudes ✓ only definition

Blessed are the poor in spirit,
   for theirs is the kingdom of heaven.
Blessed are they who mourn,
   for they will be comforted.
Blessed are the meek,
   for they will inherit the land.
Blessed are they who hunger and thirst for righteousness,
   for they will be satisfied.
Blessed are the merciful,
   for they will be shown mercy.
Blessed are the clean of heart,
   for they will see God.
Blessed are the peacemakers,
   for they will be called children of God.
Blessed are they who are persecuted for the sake of righteousness,
   for theirs is the kingdom of heaven.

—Matthew 5:3–10

Precepts of the Church

1. Take part in the Mass on Sundays and holy days.
2. Celebrate the Sacrament of Reconciliation at least once a year if there is serious sin.
3. Receive Holy Communion at least once a year during Easter time.
4. Keep holy Sundays and holy days.
5. Fast and abstain on days of penance.
6. Give your time, gifts, and money to support the Church.

Gifts of the Holy Spirit

Wisdom

Understanding

Right judgment (Counsel)

Courage (Fortitude)

Knowledge

Reverence (Piety)

Wonder and awe (Fear of the Lord)

Fruits of the Spirit

Charity	Generosity
Joy	Gentleness
Peace	Faithfulness
Patience	Modesty
Kindness	Self-control
Goodness	Chastity

Theological Virtues

Faith ✓

Hope ✓

Love ✓

Cardinal Virtues

Prudence ✓	Fortitude ✓
Justice ✓	Temperance ✓

Works of Mercy

Corporal (for the body)

Feed the hungry.

Give drink to the thirsty.

Clothe the naked.

Shelter the homeless.

Visit the sick.

Visit the imprisoned.

Bury the dead.

Spiritual (for the spirit)

Warn the sinner.

Teach the ignorant.

Counsel the doubtful.

Comfort the sorrowful.

Bear wrongs patiently.

Forgive injuries.

Pray for the living and the dead.

The Sacraments

Sacraments of Initiation	Sacraments of Healing	Sacraments of Service
Baptism ✓	Reconciliation ✓	Matrimony ✓
Confirmation ✓	Anointing of the Sick ✓	Holy Orders ✓
Eucharist ✓		

Order of the Mass

Introductory Rites

1. Entrance Song
2. Greeting
3. Rite of Blessing and Sprinkling with Holy Water *or* Penitential Rite
4. Glory to God
5. Opening Prayer

Liturgy of the Word

6. First Reading *(usually from the Old Testament)*
7. Responsorial Psalm
8. Second Reading *(from New Testament Letters)*
9. Gospel Acclamation *(Alleluia)*
10. Gospel
11. Homily
12. Profession of Faith *(Creed)*
13. General Intercessions

Liturgy of the Eucharist

14. Offertory Song *(Procession of Gifts)*
15. Preparation of the Bread and Wine
16. Invitation to Prayer
17. Prayer over the Gifts
18. Preface
19. Acclamation *(Holy, Holy, Holy Lord)*
20. Eucharistic Prayer with Acclamation
21. Great Amen

Liturgy of the Eucharist continued

Communion Rite
22. Lord's Prayer
23. Sign of Peace
24. Breaking of the Bread
25. Prayers before Communion
26. Lamb of God
27. Holy Communion
28. Communion Song
29. Silent Reflection or Song of Praise
30. Prayer after Communion

Concluding Rite
31. Greeting
32. Blessing
33. Dismissal

Holy Days

(observed in the United States)

Christmas, the Nativity of the Lord	December 25
Solemnity of Mary the Mother of God	January 1
Ascension of the Lord	40 days after Easter
✓ Assumption	August 15
All Saints' Day	November 1
Immaculate Conception	December 8

Receiving Holy Communion

To receive Holy Communion, you must be free from mortal sin. You must be sorry for any venial sin committed since your last confession. The penitential rite at the beginning of Mass is an opportunity to express your sorrow.

To honor the Lord, we fast for one hour before receiving Holy Communion. Fasting means going without food and drink, except water and medicine.

Catholics are required to receive Holy Communion at least once a year during Easter time. But it is important to receive Holy Communion often—if possible, at every Mass.

Usually, Catholics are permitted to receive Holy Communion only once a day. There are some exceptions, such as attendance at a wedding or funeral liturgy.

Examination of Conscience

1. Look at your life in the light of the Beatitudes, the Ten Commandments, the Great Commandment, and the precepts of the Church.

2. Ask yourself:
   - Where have I fallen short of what God wants for me?
   - Whom have I hurt?
   - What have I done that I knew was wrong?
   - What have I not done that I should have done?
   - Are there sins I neglected to mention the last time I confessed?
   - Have I done penance and tried as hard as I could to make up for past sins?
   - Have I made the necessary changes in bad habits?
   - What areas am I still having trouble with?
   - Am I sincerely sorry for all my sins?

3. In addition to any sins you are confessing, you may wish to talk about one or more of the above questions with the priest.

4. Pray for the Holy Spirit's help in making a fresh start.

The Sacrament of Reconciliation

Communal Rite of Reconciliation

1. Greeting
2. Reading from Scripture
3. Homily
4. Examination of Conscience *with* Litany of Contrition *and* the Lord's Prayer
5. Individual Confession and Absolution
6. Closing Prayer

Individual Rite of Reconciliation

1. Welcome
2. Reading from Scripture
3. Confession of Sins
4. Act of Contrition
5. Absolution
6. Closing Prayer

Way of the Cross

Traditional

1. Jesus is condemned to death.
2. Jesus takes up his cross.
3. Jesus falls the first time.
4. Jesus meets his sorrowful mother.
5. Simon of Cyrene helps Jesus.
6. Veronica wipes the face of Jesus.
7. Jesus falls a second time.
8. Jesus meets the women of Jerusalem.
9. Jesus falls a third time.
10. Jesus is stripped of his clothing.
11. Jesus is nailed to the cross.
12. Jesus dies on the cross.
13. Jesus' body is removed from the cross.
14. Jesus' body is placed in the tomb.

Scriptural

1. Jesus prays in the Garden of Olives.
2. Jesus is betrayed by Judas and arrested.
3. Jesus is condemned by the Sanhedrin.
4. Jesus is denied by Peter.
5. Jesus is condemned by Pontius Pilate.
6. Jesus is scourged and crowned with thorns.
7. Jesus is made to carry the cross.
8. Simon of Cyrene helps Jesus.
9. Jesus meets the women of Jerusalem.
10. Jesus is crucified.
11. Jesus promises the kingdom to the thief who repents.
12. Jesus speaks to his mother and his friend John.
13. Jesus dies on the cross.
14. Jesus is laid in the tomb.

Prayer for the Way of the Cross

We adore you, O Christ, and we bless you,
because by your holy cross you have redeemed the world.

Praying the Rosary

1. Hold the crucifix, and pray the Apostles' Creed.

2. Pray the Lord's Prayer when holding each single bead.

3. Pray the Hail Mary on each bead in a group of three or ten. A group of ten Hail Marys is called a *decade* of the Rosary. Think of one mystery as you pray each decade.

4. After every group of Hail Marys, pray Glory to the Father.

5. Close the Rosary by praying Hail, Holy Queen.

> Hail, holy Queen, mother of mercy,
> hail, our life, our sweetness, and our hope.
> To you we cry, the children of Eve;
> to you we send up our sighs,
> mourning and weeping in this land of exile.
> Turn, then, most gracious advocate,
> your eyes of mercy toward us;
> lead us home at last
> and show us the blessed fruit of your womb, Jesus:
> O clement, O loving, O sweet Virgin Mary.

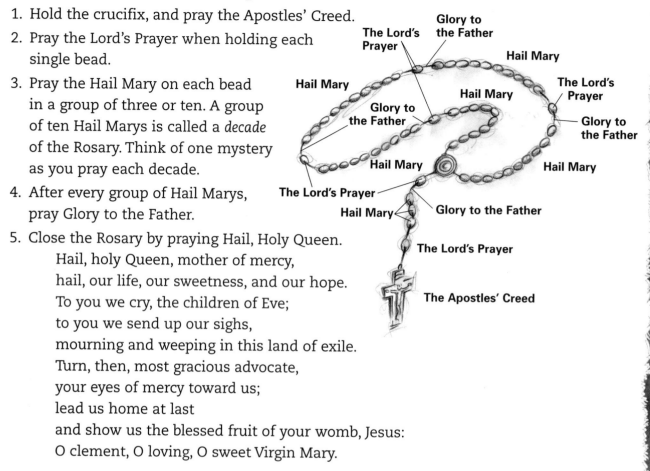

Mysteries of the Rosary

Joyful Mysteries

1. The Annunciation
2. The Visitation
3. The Nativity
4. The Presentation
5. Finding Jesus in the Temple

Sorrowful Mysteries

1. The Agony in the Garden
2. The Scourging
3. Crowning with Thorns
4. Carrying the Cross
5. The Crucifixion

Glorious Mysteries

1. The Resurrection
2. The Ascension
3. The Coming of the Holy Spirit
4. The Assumption
5. The Coronation of Mary as Queen of Heaven

THE LANGUAGE OF FAITH

A

Advent The four-week liturgical season of preparation for Christmas. The first Sunday of Advent is the beginning of the Church year. The word *Advent* means "coming."

Advent wreath An evergreen wreath in which four candles are set. One candle is lit each Sunday of Advent as special prayers are said. Traditionally the first, second, and fourth candles are violet, the color of penitence. The third candle is a lighter shade of rose to remind us of the Christmas joy we await.

ambo The lectern, or reading stand, from which the gospel is proclaimed at Mass. The ambo is sometimes called "the table of the word."

angels Pure spirits created by God to praise him and to help communicate his will to humans. The word *angel* means "messenger." Traditionally Catholics believe that God has given each of us a guardian angel to help us on our faith journey.

Anointing of the Sick The sacrament that celebrates the healing of body and spirit by Jesus. The Sacrament of Anointing can be celebrated anytime a person is seriously ill or weakened by age.

apostles The special friends and followers of Jesus to whom he entrusted his mission. According to the Gospels, there were twelve apostles (a number corresponding to the twelve tribes of Israel). The word *apostle* means "one who is sent." The teaching and ruling authority of the Church flows from Jesus through the apostles to their successors, the pope and the bishops.

apostolic In the tradition of the first and closest followers of Jesus. The Church is apostolic because it is built on the foundation of the apostles. The Church's mission is that of Jesus, continued through the apostles and their successors, the bishops.

ascension Jesus' return to his Father in heaven after his resurrection. We celebrate the Feast of the Ascension as a holy day 40 days after Easter. The word *ascension* means "rising."

assumption The mystery of Mary's being taken to heaven body and soul at the end of her life. The Feast of the Assumption, a holy day, is celebrated on August 15.

B

Baptism The first sacrament we celebrate. Baptism makes us children of God and members of the Church by making us members of the Body of Christ. It takes away original sin and all personal sin.

Beatitudes Sayings of Jesus (*Matthew 5:3–10*) that sum up the way to live in God's kingdom and that point the way to true happiness. The word *beatitude* means "blessedness."

Bible God's word written down by humans; the Church's holy book, also called *Scripture*. The Bible is made up of many different books in two parts, the Old Testament and the New Testament. The word *bible* means "library."

bishop A man ordained to lead and teach the followers of Jesus. The bishops are successors of the apostles. A bishop or *archbishop* usually leads a group of parishes called a *diocese* or *archdiocese*. The word *bishop* means "overseer."

C

canonization The process by which the Catholic Church formally recognizes a deceased person as a saint. Once that person's virtues are publicly recognized, he or she is given a place in the Church's official calendar, or *canon*, of feast days. Many saints of the early Church, and other holy men and women of later years, are not canonized, but we celebrate their virtues with those of all other holy men and women on November 1, the Feast of All Saints.

cantor The liturgical minister who leads the community in sacred song.

cardinal virtues Prudence, justice, fortitude, and temperance are the four habits of goodness from which all other human virtues flow. They are called *cardinal*, or "hinge," virtues because other virtues depend on them.

catechumenate The period of preparation, including study and prayer, for the celebration of the Sacraments of Initiation. A person preparing to celebrate these sacraments is called a *catechumen*, or "learner."

catholic A word that means "universal." The Church is catholic because its mission is to the whole world.

celibacy The state of being unmarried for the sake of the kingdom of God. In the Western Church priests and bishops are bound to celibacy, as are deacons who are unmarried at the time of their ordination, or who become widowed after ordination.

chastity The virtue that directs us to use God's gift of sexuality properly. All people are called to practice the virtue of chastity according to their states of life.

chrism Sacred oil, made from olive oil scented with spices, used for anointing in the Sacraments of Baptism, Confirmation, and Holy Orders. In Eastern Rite Churches, Confirmation takes its name from this anointing and is known as *Chrismation*.

Christians People who follow Jesus Christ. Christians are baptized in the name of the Father, the Son, and the Holy Spirit. The word *Christian* comes from *Christ*, which means "anointed one."

Christmas The holy day that celebrates the birth of Jesus, the Son of God who became human to save us from the power of sin and everlasting death. The name *Christmas* comes from the words "Christ's Mass."

Church The community of all baptized people who believe in God and follow Jesus. A *church* is also the name of the building where we gather to worship God.

commandments Laws given by God to humans as a sign of the covenant. We are most familiar with the laws known as the *Ten Commandments*, which tell of our responsibilities to God and our neighbor.

compassion The merciful quality of sharing the sufferings of another.

Confirmation The Sacrament of Initiation that seals and completes Baptism. In Confirmation we are sealed with the Holy Spirit.

conscience The gift from God that helps us know the difference between right and wrong and choose what is right. Conscience is free will and reason working together. We must form our conscience properly. We *examine*, or check, our conscience in preparation for the Sacrament of Reconciliation.

consecrated Set apart for special, holy use. At Mass, when the bread and wine are consecrated, they become the Body and Blood of Jesus Christ.

contemplative A style of religious life centered on solitude and prayer, especially the kind of prayer that leads to *contemplation*, or focusing on God's presence. Contemplative religious communities may also be called *cloistered*, or "walled," because their members choose to live apart from the outside world.

contrition The sorrow we feel when we have sinned. Contrition moves us to seek forgiveness and to change our lives for the better. *Perfect contrition* is based solely on sorrow for having damaged our relationships with God and others, without any thought of the punishment that sin deserves.

conversion The process of turning away from sin and evil and turning toward God. Jesus announced his ministry by calling all people to conversion.

covenant A sacred promise or agreement joining God and humans in relationship. God made a covenant with the people of Israel and renewed it often. Jesus' sacrifice established the new and everlasting covenant, open to all who do God's will.

creation All things that exist, seen or unseen. God made all creation from nothing and sustains creation with his love. God entrusted the care of creation to us. At the end of time, all creation will be transformed by the coming of God's kingdom in its fullness.

creed A formal statement of what we believe. The word *creed* comes from the Latin for "I believe." The two most familiar creeds are the Apostles' Creed and the Nicene Creed, which we proclaim at Mass.

D

deacon A man who is ordained to serve the Church by baptizing, proclaiming the gospel, preaching, witnessing marriages, and doing works of charity.

devotions Individual or group nonliturgical practices that show love for God, Mary, and the saints. The Rosary and Way of the Cross are examples of Catholic devotions.

diocese The area overseen by a bishop. A diocese is usually made up of a number of parishes. A large diocese may be known as an *archdiocese*, overseen by an archbishop.

divine Godlike. Jesus is both human and divine. Because we are made in God's image, we, too, have the divine presence within us. Our call is to turn away from sin and to grow more and more like God.

doctrine Official Church teaching about the truths of our faith. The word *doctrine* means "teaching."

E

Easter The Feast of the Resurrection of Jesus Christ, our greatest holy day. In the northern hemisphere, Easter is celebrated in the springtime. The exact date changes every year.

Easter Vigil The liturgical celebration that takes place on Holy Saturday night. This great feast includes the Service of Light (blessing the new fire and welcoming the Paschal candle), the Service of the Word (readings and songs recalling God's faithfulness to the covenant), the celebration of the Sacraments of Initiation, and the Eucharistic celebration of the Feast of the Resurrection.

elect Those candidates who have been approved by the community to receive the Sacraments of Initiation, usually at the Easter Vigil. The word *elect* means "chosen."

epiphany The Greek word for "manifestation" or "revelation." The Feast of the Epiphany, celebrated on the Sunday closest to January 6, recalls the visit of the magi to the Child Jesus, who was revealed to be the Savior of the world.

Eucharist The sacrament of Jesus' presence under the form of bread and wine. We receive Jesus' own Body and Blood as Holy Communion during the Eucharistic celebration. The word *Eucharist* means "thanksgiving."

Eucharistic assembly The Church; the gathering of all members of the worshiping community to offer thanks and praise to God at Mass.

evangelical counsels Vows of poverty, chastity, and obedience taken by members of religious communities. They are called *evangelical counsels*, or "advice based on the gospel," because they sum up the gospel way of life.

evil The absence of the divine goodness that God built into creation. Evil is the result of the choice to disobey God. With suffering and death evil is one of the lasting effects of original sin.

Exodus The Israelites' journey from slavery in Egypt to freedom in the promised land, accomplished and directed by God. The account of this journey is found in the biblical Book of Exodus. It forms the basis of the Jewish feast of Passover. The word *exodus* means "going out."

F

faith The gift given to us by God that moves us to seek him out and believe in him. Faith, hope, and love, are the three *theological*, or God-given, virtues.

fortitude The cardinal virtue that helps us act with courage to do what is right. Fortitude, sometimes known as courage, is one of the gifts of the Holy Spirit.

free will The God-given ability to choose between good and evil.

G

Genesis The first book of the Bible, which tells of God's creation of the world and his covenants with our ancestors in faith. The word *genesis* means "beginning" or "origin."

gifts of the Holy Spirit The seven powerful gifts received in Baptism and strengthened in Confirmation. They are wisdom, understanding, counsel (right judgment), fortitude (courage), knowledge, piety (reverence), and fear of the Lord (wonder and awe). These gifts help us grow in our relationships with God and others.

God The one, true, divine Being to whom all creation owes worship and glory. God is all-good, all-powerful, all-knowing, eternal, and completely merciful. God created and sustains all things. From the beginning of time, God has revealed himself to humans, who could not otherwise come to know him. The most complete revelation of God is Jesus Christ, who showed us that God is the Holy Trinity of Father, Son, and Holy Spirit.

godparent A person who agrees to sponsor someone who is to be baptized. For a child the family and godparents are responsible for helping the child grow in his or her Catholic faith. The whole Church community stands with the godparents in taking on this responsibility.

gospel A word that means "good news." The gospel message is the good news of God's reign and saving love. In the New Testament, the four stories of Jesus' life and teachings are called the *Gospels*.

grace God's free, unlimited, loving gift of his own self to humans. Grace is not a thing, but a relationship. We grow in grace by participating in the sacraments and living faithful, loving, and holy lives.

H

heaven Being with God forever. Heaven is not a place but a state of being. Through God's grace heaven is our destined home. It is complete, unending joy.

Hebrew Scriptures The books of the Bible recognized by the Jewish community as having been inspired by God, used in Jewish prayer and worship. The Old Testament of the Christian Bible is made up of the Hebrew Scriptures and other pre-Christian writings considered inspired by the Church.

hell Eternal separation from God, the consequence of deliberately rejecting God's merciful love and forgiveness. Hell is not a place but a state of being. Its greatest punishment is the separation from God and from all those who share God's friendship.

holy days Special feast days of the Church. We celebrate holy days just as we do Sundays, by participating at Mass and by setting aside time to rest and pray.

Holy Orders The sacrament by which men are ordained to serve God and the Church as deacons, priests, or bishops.

Holy Spirit The third Person of the Holy Trinity. The Holy Spirit is God's own love and holiness present with us in the Church. Jesus promised that the Holy Spirit would help his followers. The Holy Spirit is one with the Father and the Son.

Holy Trinity The mystery of one God in three Persons: Father, Son, and Holy Spirit. This mystery was revealed to us by Jesus.

homily A talk given by the presider, deacon, or special homilist during the Liturgy of the Word at Mass. The homily, sometimes called a *sermon*, helps the assembly understand and apply the Scripture readings.

I

image of God The divine likeness in each person, the result of having been created by God. Our belief that all people are made in God's image calls us to show honor and respect for the dignity of each person.

immortal Not subject to death. The soul, the divine life within us, is immortal and lives forever.

incarnation The mystery of the immortal Son of God becoming human in Jesus Christ for our sake. The word *incarnation* means "taking on flesh."

infallible Always true and right. Because the Holy Spirit guides the Church, the Church's teaching is infallible in certain matters of faith and morals when the pope and the bishops in union with the pope so declare.

initiation The process of becoming a member of the Church. The Sacraments of Baptism, Confirmation, and Eucharist are Sacraments of Initiation, necessary for entering fully into the life of the Church.

inspired Moved and guided by the Holy Spirit. We believe that the authors of Scripture were inspired. The Bible is truly God's word, spoken in the words of humans.

intercede To act on someone else's behalf. We ask Mary and the saints to intercede for us with God. When we ask God's help for someone else, we are practicing the prayer of intercession.

J

Jesus A name that means "God saves." We believe that Jesus is both God and human. He taught us about God, his Father. He suffered, died, and was raised from death to save us from the power of sin and everlasting death.

justice The cardinal virtue that helps us carry out our moral obligations toward others. Justice is giving each person what he or she is due, not based on material standing or merit, but simply because he or she is a child of God. We work for social justice on earth as a sign of the everlasting justice of God's reign.

K

kingdom of God God's reign of justice, love, and peace. Jesus came to bring the kingdom of God, which is both present in our midst and yet to come. All creation will be transformed when the kingdom of God comes in its fullness.

L

last rites The rituals celebrated by Catholics at the time of death to help us move from our earthly life to everlasting life with God. The last rites include the Sacrament of Anointing, the Sacrament of Reconciliation, and reception of the Eucharist as *viaticum*.

lay People who are not ordained. The word *lay* means "the people."

lectionary The book of Scripture readings used at Mass. The lectionary readings for Sunday Masses are organized into a three-year repeating cycle. Over the course of the cycle, the assembly hears a great portion of the Bible.

lector A liturgical minister who proclaims God's word at Mass or in other liturgical settings. The word *lector* means "reader."

Lent The liturgical season of preparation for Easter. Lent begins on Ash Wednesday and lasts approximately 40 days. The Season of Lent is a time for prayer, penance, and acts of charity. It is also the time of final retreat and preparation for those who will celebrate the Sacraments of Initiation at the Easter Vigil. The word *Lent* means "spring," the season during which Lent falls in the northern hemisphere.

litany A series of brief prayers of petition or intercession, each followed by a repeated response. The general intercessions at Mass are in the form of a litany.

liturgical minister A lay person who carries out various ministries during the celebration of the liturgy. Lectors, cantors, altar servers, ushers, choir members and musicians, extraordinary ministers of the Eucharist, and greeters are all liturgical ministers.

liturgy The public prayer and worship of the Church. The Eucharistic celebration is the highest form of liturgy. The word *liturgy* means "the work of the people."

M

magi The astrologers or wise men who came from the East to acknowledge Jesus as the King of the Jews. Their visit remembered at the Feast of the Epiphany. The magi are sometimes called the *Three Kings* and are traditionally given the names Balthasar, Melchior, and Gaspar. They are often shown as representing the various ages and races of humanity.

magisterium The teaching authority of the Catholic Church, exercised by the bishops and the pope in service to the word of God. The Holy Spirit guides and directs these successors of the apostles. *Magisterium* means "body of teachers."

marks of the Church The identifying characteristics of the presence of the Holy Spirit in the Church. The Church is one, holy, catholic, and apostolic.

Mary The mother of Jesus. We believe that Mary was free from original sin and all personal sin from the very beginning of her life. We believe that she remained a virgin throughout her life. And we believe that God took her to be with him forever, body and soul, at the time of her death. Mary is the Mother of the Church, and our mother, too.

Mass The celebration of the Eucharistic liturgy. Catholics are obliged to attend Mass on Sundays and holy days. The word *Mass* means "dismissal." At the end of Mass, we are dismissed, or sent out into the world, to live our faith every day.

Matrimony The sacrament that joins a man and a woman in Christian marriage.

meditate To pray quietly by reflecting on a passage of Scripture or silently praying a repeated prayer. When a prayer leader directs a group to meditate on a series of images or passages, the experience is called a *guided meditation*.

messiah The Hebrew word for "anointed, or chosen, one." Old Testament prophets spoke of a messiah who would lead Israel back into God's favor. Christians believe that Jesus is the Messiah sent to bring all people into God's everlasting kingdom. The title *Christ* means *messiah*.

miracle A deed of great power, outside the abilities of nature. Jesus performed miracles, not to show off his own power but to testify to God's all-powerful love and mercy.

morality The way we put our beliefs into action for good. The heart of our Christian morality is the Great Commandment to love God above all things and our neighbor as ourselves. The word of God in Scripture, the life of Jesus, the Ten Commandments, the Beatitudes, the teachings of the Church, and the examples of faithful people are all sources of our morality.

mystery A truth of our faith that we cannot fully understand but that we believe because God has shown it to us in Scripture, in the life of Jesus, or in the teachings of the Church. The Holy Trinity is a mystery.

N

New Testament The second part of the Bible. The New Testament is the story of Jesus and his followers. It contains the four Gospels, an account of the early Church, a number of letters, or *epistles*, and the Book of Revelation.

O

Old Testament The first part of the Bible. The Old Testament tells the story of the Jewish people before Jesus was born. The Old Testament is made up of the *Pentateuch* or *Torah*, the prophetic books, and other writings such as religious histories and wisdom literature.

ordained Called forth to serve God and the Church through the Sacrament of Holy Orders. Deacons, priests, and bishops are ordained men.

original sin The human condition of weakness and tendency toward sin that resulted from the first humans' choice to disobey God. Only Jesus, the Son of God, and Mary, his mother, were free of original sin. Baptism restores the relationship of loving grace in which all people were created by God. But the temptation remains to choose what we want rather than what God wants.

P

pall A white cloth used to cover the coffin at a funeral Mass. It is a sign of the white garment of Baptism. The word *pall* means "cloak."

parable A special kind of teaching story often used by Jesus to describe God's kingdom and explain God's will for us. Parables feature brief, dramatic stories that often end unexpectedly, challenging the listener to search for the deeper meaning.

Paschal mystery The saving mystery of Jesus' suffering, death, and resurrection. We celebrate the Paschal mystery at every Eucharist. The word *Paschal* refers to the Hebrew word for Passover, the feast that celebrates God's saving love for the people of Israel. Jesus' sacrifice extended that love and salvation to all people.

patron A saint or angel chosen to intercede for and help an individual, group, or nation. Traditionally a Catholic is given the name of a saint at Baptism, and this saint is asked to watch over the person. Under the title of the Immaculate Conception, Mary is the patron of the United States.

penance Prayers and actions undertaken to make up for the harm our sins have caused. In the Sacrament of Reconciliation, the priest gives us a penance, also called *satisfaction*, to do. The liturgy of the Sacrament of Reconciliation is called the *Rite of Penance*. We also do penance at other times, especially during the liturgical Season of Lent.

pope The visible leader of the Catholic Church on earth. The pope is the bishop of Rome. He follows in the footsteps of Saint Peter, whom Jesus chose to lead his followers. The pope acts with the bishops to teach and guide the Church in service to the word of God.

prayer Talking to and listening to God. Prayer can be private or public; spoken, sung, or silent; formal or spontaneous. The five reasons for prayer are blessing and adoration, petition, intercession, thanksgiving, and praise.

precepts of the Church Some of the important duties of Catholics. The word *precept* means "teaching" or "guidance."

presider The priest or bishop who leads the assembly in the Eucharistic celebration. Only a priest or bishop may preside at Mass and consecrate the Eucharist. In parishes where no presider is available for Sunday Mass, a deacon or liturgical minister may lead a Service of the Word and distribute Holy Communion, using the reserved Blessed Sacrament.

priest A man who is ordained to serve God and the Church by celebrating the sacraments, preaching, and presiding at Mass.

prophet A person called by God to speak God's message to humans. The word *prophet* means "to speak before." Prophets often call people to turn from evil and warn them of the consequences of sin. Every baptized Christian is called to share in the ministry of the prophet.

providence God's loving care for all things; God's will and plan for creation.

prudence The cardinal virtue that helps us choose what is morally right, with the help of the Holy Spirit and our own educated conscience. Prudence is at the heart of all moral decisions.

R

Reconciliation The sacrament that celebrates God's forgiveness of sin through the Church. This sacrament is also known as *Penance*. The word *reconciliation* means "coming back together" or "making peace."

Redeemer A title of Jesus that expresses our belief that by his suffering, death, and resurrection he won for us freedom from the power of sin and everlasting death. To *redeem* means to "buy back," to "ransom," or to "rescue."

reign Another word for kingdom or power. God's reign is a kingdom of justice, love, and peace, announced by Jesus Christ, present in our midst, and yet to come in fullness.

religious communities Groups of men or women who make promises to serve God and the Church through lives of prayer and action. Members of religious communities make vows of poverty, chastity, and obedience. Members are known as religious priests, sisters, nuns, brothers, monks, or friars.

repentance The desire to turn away from sin and return to loving relationships with God and others.

resurrection The mystery of Jesus being raised from death by God's loving power. We celebrate the Feast of the Resurrection at Easter.

revelation The process by which God chooses to make himself known to us. The chief sources of revelation are God's creation, the Scriptures, the teachings of the Church, and the liturgical celebrations of the sacraments. All of these are summed up in Jesus Christ, the most perfect revelation of God.

reverence The deep honor and respect we owe to God, and, by extension, to all that God has made. Reverence, sometimes called *piety*, is one of the gifts of the Holy Spirit.

righteousness Moral conduct that is in keeping with the will of God; holiness.

Rosary A form of prayer to Mary. We pray Hail Marys, usually counting off the prayers on a circle of beads. While we pray, we keep in mind important events in the lives of Jesus and his mother. We call these events *mysteries of the Rosary.*

S

sacraments Celebrations in which Jesus joins with the assembled community in liturgical actions that are signs and sources of God's grace. We celebrate seven sacraments: Baptism, Confirmation, Eucharist (Sacraments of Initiation); Reconciliation, the Anointing of the Sick (Sacraments of Healing); Matrimony, and Holy Orders (Sacraments of Service). The word *sacrament* means "seal." The sacraments seal our relationships with God and the Christian community.

sacred Holy; set aside for God's service.

sacrifice To give up something for a greater good; something precious offered completely to God. Jesus offered himself as a sacrifice on the cross to save us from the power of sin and everlasting death. We celebrate this sacrifice at every Mass.

saint Holy one; someone whose life bears special witness to the gospel message. Saints are people of all ages, national origins, and walks of life. Saints are happy forever with God. The Church honors the saints by celebrating their feast days and by asking for their prayers.

sanctified Made holy. The Holy Spirit sanctifies the members of the Church.

Seder The special meal with which Jewish people celebrate the feast of Passover. The foods symbolize events associated with the Israelites' passage from slavery to freedom. Jesus and his friends celebrated a Seder on the night before he died.

sin The choice to disobey God. Sin can be serious (mortal) or less serious (venial). Sin is a deliberate choice, not a mistake or an accident. God forgives us when we are truly sorry.

soul The immortal part of our being; God's life in us. The human person is a unity of body and soul.

sponsor A representative of the Christian community who is a witness to the commitment of an older child or adult celebrating the Sacraments of Initiation.

stewardship Responsible care for creation. God has entrusted all creation to our stewardship.

T

temperance The cardinal virtue that helps us practice *moderation*, or balance, in our lives.

Ten Commandments The *Decalogue*, or "ten words," summing up God's laws given as part of the covenant at Sinai. The first three commandments sum up

our responsibilities to God. The next seven commandments sum up our responsibilities to our neighbor.

Tradition The entirety of the word of God entrusted to the apostles by Christ and the Holy Spirit and passed on through the successors of the apostles, the bishops.

Passed on

V

viaticum Holy Communion received as part of the last rites at the time of death. The word *viaticum* means "bread for the journey."

virtue A habit or practice of goodness that helps us grow in love for God and others. There are three theological virtues—faith, hope, and love—and four cardinal virtues—prudence, justice, fortitude, and temperance.

vocation The desire to follow a particular state of life in response to God's call. *Vocation* means "calling." All Christians have vocations by virtue of their Baptism. Religious life, priesthood, marriage, and single life are ways of answering God's call.

vows Sacred promises made to God. Catholics make public vows in the Sacraments of Baptism, Matrimony, and Holy Orders. Members of religious communities also make public vows.

W

works of mercy Actions that show justice, love, and peace, as Jesus did. The Corporal Works of Mercy are actions that care for the physical needs of others. The Spiritual Works of Mercy are actions that care for the spiritual needs of others.

worship Public honor shown to God in prayer and liturgy. Worship is a natural response to God's loving goodness.

INDEX

Boldfaced numbers refer to pages on which the terms are defined.

Body and Blood of, 175, 177, 206
death and resurrection of, 174, 182, 194–201
divinity of, 69
as God's Word, 68
healing signs of, 143
images of, 71
as Jew, 187
Mary as mother of, 33
    See also Mary, Mother of God
miracles of, 76
parables and stories of, 74–81
Paschal mystery of, 86
Passover of, 182–185, 197
presence in the Blessed Sacrament, 179
as Prince of Peace, 130
receiving in Eucharist, 174
resurrection of, 33, **85**, 213
return of, 205, 207
as Savior, 105, 123–124, 173
as second Person of the Holy Trinity, 46
as Son of God, 25, 54, 68–70
Jewish people, 186–193, 206
bonds of faith with, 187
major feasts celebrated by, 191
reading of Scripture by, 166
Sabbath blessings of, 176
sufferings of, 190
    See also Israelites
John, Saint, 85
John the Baptist, 54, 98, 123
John Chrysostom, Saint, 47
John of Damascus, Saint, 70
John Paul II, Pope, 190
Joseph, Saint, 69, 165, 187
judgment, 136
justice, 77, **136**, 138, 205

K

Katharine Drexel, Blessed, 99
kingdom of God, **76**–78, 98, 126–133, 196, 198–199, 202–209
    See also reign

L

last rites, **198**
Last Supper, 174, 176
lay, **114**
lectionary, **167**, 170
lectors, **160**
Lent, **152**–155, 169
litany, **65**
liturgical ministers, **160**
liturgy, **46**–47, 50–51, 165 See also Eucharist, Sacrament of; Mass; sacraments; worship
Liturgy of the Eucharist, 176–177, 199, 224
Liturgy of the Hours, **119**
Liturgy of the Word, 167–171, 199, 224
Lord's Prayer, 26, 78, 177
love, God's, 14–21, 69, 71, 73, 129

M

magi, **122**
magisterium, **100**
Marcion, 164–165, 169
Margaret of Scotland, Saint, 116
marks of the Church, **98**–103

Martin de Porres, Saint, 136
Mary, Mother of God, 33, 69, 83, 165 187
celebrating, 32–35
at Jesus' birth, 122–123
visit to Elizabeth, 137
Mass, **43**, 46, 48, 163
concluding rite, 177, 224
Holy Spirit's presence at, 175
introductory rites, 168, 224
Liturgy of the Eucharist, 176–177, 224
Liturgy of the Word, 169, 224
order of, 224–225
participating in, 47
preparing for, 161
roles at, 160
Scripture readings at, 166
Matrimony, Sacrament of, 87, 114, 117–118
meditation, **41**
Messiah, **93**, 98, 186–187
    See also Jesus Christ
miracles, **76**, 80–81
Miriam, 193
morality, **130**–132, 141
Moses, 191, 193

N

Native Americans, 23, 99
new covenant, 182–183
new creation, 32–35
new earth, 203
new heaven, 203
new Jerusalem, 204–205
new life, 52, 82–89, 105, 197
Newman, Cardinal John Henry, 73
New Testament, 164–167, 169
    See also Bible; Gospels; Scripture
Nicene Creed, 169, 215
Nicodemus, 105

O

obligation, 160
Old Testament, 164–167, 169, 187
    See also Bible; Hebrew Scriptures
ordained, **114**–115, 118
original sin, **18**, 70, 82, 108

P

pall, **198**
parables, **77**, 79–80
parish, 43, 63
Paschal mystery, **86**–87, 176, 213
Passover, 86, 182–185, 191–192, 197
Patrick, Saint, 15
patron saints, 63–64
Paul, Saint, 85, 99, 158–159, 165, 169, 196, 207
peace, 57, 77, 130, 205
penance, Lenten, 152–154
    See also Reconciliation
Pentecost, **59**, 191
Peter, Saint, 85, 98, 165
pope, 100
prayer, 41, 44–51, **45**
    See also individual prayers, 216–220, 227–228
precepts of the Church, 223
priest, 111, 114–115, 117, 147, 160

prophet, **54**, 93, 98
providence, **24**–25, 27–28
prudence, **136**
psalms, 43, 119, 163, 167–169, 187

R

Reconciliation, Sacrament of, 87, 93, 143–147, 149, 198, 226
redeemer, **83**
reign, 77, 98, 131, **203**–204
    See also kingdom of God
religious life, 114
repentance, 78
resurrection, 33, **85**, 88, 174, 182, 194–201, 213
revelation, **14**
righteousness, **129**
Rome, 63, 164

S

sacraments, **55**, 84, 166, 197, 205, 213, 224
Church as, 98
Jesus as, 71
Paschal mystery and, 87
    See also individual sacraments
sacred, **159**
sacrifice, 93, 182
saint, **62**–65
    See also individual saints
salvation, 176, 183, 196, 203, 207
Salve, Regina, 35
sanctified, **55**
Savior, 105, 123
Scripture, 11, 43, 79, 93, 107, 165–167, 187 See also Bible; New Testament; Old Testament
second coming, 93, 205, 207
Seder, **188**
Service, Sacraments of, 114, 117
Sign of the Cross, 47, 73, 169
Simeon, 69
sin, **18**, 70, 78, 143, 149, 152, 168, 203, 206
soul, **33**–34
sponsor, **107**
stewardship, **26**, 28
suffering, 18, 82–83, 86, 88, 146, 203

T

temperance, **137**
temple, 204
theological virtues, 223
Thomas Aquinas, Saint, 185
Thomas More, Saint, 136
Tradition, **166**
Triduum, 182, 184

U

unity, **100**, 158

V

Vatican councils, 100
viaticum, **198**
virtue, **135**–141
vocation, **112**–118
vows, **115**

W

wisdom, 135, 137, 141
works of mercy, 86, 205, 223
worship, 44–51, **45**